Dear Diary

Mandy Claridge

authorHOUSE®

AuthorHouse™
1663 Liberty Drive
Bloomington, IN 47403
www.authorhouse.com
Phone: 1-800-839-8640

First published by AuthorHouse 03/21/2011

ISBN: 978-1-4567-4689-6 (sc)
ISBN: 978-1-4567-4688-9 (e-b)

Library of Congress Control Number: 2011904571

Printed in the United States of America

*Any people depicted in stock imagery provided by Thinkstock are models,
and such images are being used for illustrative purposes only.
Certain stock imagery © Thinkstock.*

This book is printed on acid-free paper.

I n early October, Laney Cole sat at her kitchen table reading the *Daily Times* newspaper. She was a full-time student at Rutgers University, studying poetry, and she worked part time as a hair dresser at a local salon near her house. Laney had honey-blonde hair that matched her golden brown eyes.

It was a sunny, fall morning, and the voice of Louis Armstrong singing "What A Wonderful World" came out of the radio on the countertop. Laney flipped through the newspaper to see what was going on in the world when she turned to the obituary section. Her heart stopped for a moment when she read her best friend's name in bold, black letters: **Sandra Lynn Kean.** Laney remembered the way she had found her friend. She read the obituary:

Sandra Lynn Kean
1981–2008

Sandra Lynn Kean was a teacher at Cloudsdale

Elementary School. She lived a simple life, with no children and one surviving relative, a brother, Scott Kean.

Laney leaned back in her chair as she wiped a tear from her eyes. She had a flashback of Sandra, face-down on her desk, with a picture in one hand and an envelope in the other. Laney's best friend was dead.

She could still hear Sandra's last words from the night she took her life: "Let you be loved before you can love another." Sandra had said this as she walked towards her bedroom. It was the last time she was seen alive. Laney didn't understand why Sandra had taken her own life.

Although it was never proven, Laney knew better. By the way, she found Sandra, face down on the desk. Laney knew her friend had planned on doing what she did. Laney had always thought that Sandra was happy and got along with everyone she had met. So why the sudden tragedy? It was a mystery to Laney.

Laney wiped the tears that began to fall, cleared her throat, and folded the newspaper. She couldn't stop wondering why her best friend had committed suicide. She was haunted by it. Laney decided that no matter what, she had to figure out what had been going through Sandra's head to make her do what she did. She didn't know how she was going to solve this mystery, but somehow she had to.

Sandra Kean had it all. She was very smart

and successful at her teaching career. She was very pretty, with her long, flowing, golden-red hair that hung past her waist. Her eyes were the color of the ocean after a rainstorm. Her teeth were perfect, and she had an inviting, accepting smile. Sandra was a slim five-foot-three. *Why would a woman with all this going take her own life?* Laney wondered.

Laney envied Sandra but never let on that she did. They had been best friends since they were kids and were in the same class all the way through high school. After college, the two girls rented a two-floor brownstone apartment in Halden, New Jersey, with a nice view of the park. The downstairs had a living room, a small dining area, and a den that they used for storage. The upstairs had a kitchen, a full bathroom, another living room, and two bedrooms. The neighbors were very nice. It was definitely an address out on easy street.

Although Laney loved this apartment, she couldn't bear to stay in it after Sandra's suicide. Too many memories, mostly good, were affected by that bad one. Laney's biggest task—and the hardest one, she thought—was cleaning out Sandra's room. Doing so would make the whole thing a reality and not just a nightmare that kept repeating. That room alone contained so many memories of her friend; packing it up was like saying good-bye forever. But what was she supposed to do? It had to be done. Laney knew she wouldn't be able to hold it together while cleaning the room, so she waited until she couldn't anymore to pack everything up.

It had been about two weeks since Laney had found Sandra. It seemed like yesterday they were all standing in the misty rain at the cemetery while the priest said his last prayer and Sandra's coffin went slowly into the ground. The hardest part for Laney had been coming home to where her friend would no longer step foot again. She knew she had to get out of that place ASAP.

Laney hesitated to open the door to Sandra's room. She took a deep breath and walked in. A gust of wind came at her as she turned on the light. Laney got a chill, shut the light, and walked out quickly. Closing the door, she realized she couldn't do this on her own. She entered the kitchen, and the thought occurred to her that maybe Scott, Sandra's brother, could help her. After all, he was her only living relative. He may want to keep something of hers. Laney hadn't spoken to Scott since the funeral and wasn't sure how to approach him. The best way, maybe, was to get right to the point.

After an hour of debating whether to call Scott or not, Laney went in search of Sandra's cell phone. It was plugged in by the lamp in the living room, where Sandra had left it. Laney unplugged the red Blackberry and scanned through the contact list until she came to Scott's name. Laney picked up the house phone and hesitated before dialing his number. She dialed and took a deep breath before the last digit.

The phone rang four times. A quiet voice answered, "Hello."

Without realizing it, a smile came over Laney's face. She had always had a thing for Scott, even when she was a kid. After a moment's pause, she said, "Hi, Scott. It's me, Laney."

"Well, if it isn't little Laney Cole. How are ya?" Scott asked.

"Um, I'm okay, I guess. I called to ask you to do me a big favor."

"Sure, what can I do for you?"

Laney hated to ask, but she had to. "Will you help me clean out Sandra's room? I plan on moving in two weeks and haven't done it yet. I can't bring myself to do it alone."

he wasn't so quick to answer this time. In a low tone, he responded "Sure, no problem. What day do you need me there?"

Now would be nice, Laney thought. "How is Saturday at noon?"

"Sounds good. I'll be there, Laney; don't worry." He hung up.

2

It seemed like forever before Saturday arrived. A three-day wait for this chore to get done might as well have been a year. Laney paced nervously as she waited for Scott to get there. She dreaded having to get rid of Sandra's stuff. It was only nine in the morning, and she still had three hours before Scott would arrive. She started to pack up the rest of the living room. She had butterflies in her stomach from just thinking about Scott arriving soon. She couldn't wait to see his boyish smile, which went perfectly with the way he wore his dirty-blonde hair. And, oh god, his hazel eyes were mesmerizing. He was a six-foot-one hottie, and he was going to be here any minute now.

The sound of the buzzer made Laney jump. She felt like she had to puke as she walked to the door. As she opened it, a warm feeling came over her face. Scott had a single red rose in his hand. "Hi," she managed to say after swallowing the lump in her throat. "Is this for me?" She reached for the rose.

Laney led him into the apartment and said in a shy voice, "Thanks for the rose. It was really sweet of you. Don't mind the mess; everything is kind of everywhere." In the living room, there were boxes piled high and the walls were bare.

Scott looked around the room. "Wow, you weren't playing when you said you were moving. You even packed up the nails that held up your pictures." He walked over to Laney, who was standing in the middle of the living room with a dazed look on her face. "So, you ready to get started?" he asked.

As they neared Sandra's room, Laney felt a huge lump in her throat. The day had come to clean out what used to be her best friend's room. She hoped that she would be able to get through it without making a big fuss in front of Scott. Laney took a deep breath as Scott opened the bedroom door. Within seconds, they were standing in the quiet room. After about a minute, Scott broke the silence. "My sister wasn't very neat. This place looks worse than my house."

There were dirty clothes tossed all over the floor and empty water bottles on her desk, dresser, and nightstand. Her clean clothes stuck out of her open dresser drawers. The wastepaper basket overflowed with crumpled pieces of paper. Sandra's bed was unmade, and the pillows were on the floor.

Laney noticed a picture on top of Sandra's tall dresser, which had empty water bottles on it as well. She walked over to examine the picture more closely. It was Sandra standing next to a

7

billboard that read, "Someday, love will come." *Very bizarre*, Laney thought as she set down the golden Tiffany frame.

"I'll get some drinks," Laney said to Scott. "I have a feeling we are going to be in here for a while." Scott nodded in agreement as she exited the room. Laney brought back two glasses of iced tea and garbage bags. She set the glasses on the nightstand and tossed the garbage bags on the floor. She sat on the bed, taking a heart-shaped pillow in her hands. The pillow had the words "friends forever" in glitter on it. Laney had given that pillow to Sandra for her birthday.

That room contained a lot of memories. Laney thought of the times they had shared, and tears filled her eyes. One time stuck out the most in Laney's mind. Sandra had come home after being out with Todd, a guy she used to date. He had cheated on her, and Sandra came home crying and very upset. Laney grabbed a gallon of ice cream and two spoons and then followed Sandra into her room. After eating half the ice cream, Sandra had calmed down and taken her garbage can from next to her desk and put it in the middle of the floor.

Sandra went around the room grabbing everything that Todd had ever given her and putting it in the garbage can. Letters, pictures, stuffed animals, all she could find, and set it on fire. The girls laughed. "Bye-bye, Todd," Sandra said as she poured water into the garbage can. That was the last guy Sandra had been with. Laney had tried to get her to go out on a few dates, but Sandra had always turned it down, saying she wasn't ready.

"Are you okay? Um ... hello? Earth to Laney," Scott said as he put some stuff into a pile.

Laney came back to reality. "Yeah, sorry, I was just thinking of the times your sister and I had in this room." She put the pillow down and got up from the bed.

"You really miss her, don't you?" Scott said looking deeply at her.

"Yeah, I do. It just doesn't seem real to me." Laney picked up some of the dirty clothes off the floor and was sort of folding them. "What do you think about donating her clothes to Goodwill?"

"I think that is exactly what my sister would've wanted," Scott said with a smile.

Laney liked the way how Scott was always calm and cool about everything. He was the type that went with the flow in any situation. It made her believe that there wasn't any point in dwelling in the past. It only kept you from moving on to the future.

After two hours, they had two huge bags of garbage and one bag for Goodwill. Laney glanced up at Scott. "Are you hungry? Want to take a break and have some lunch?"

"Sure thing. I never pass up food," he said with a boyish smile.

They reached for the doorknob at the same time, causing them to bump into each other. As their eyes met, they giggled a little. Scott opened the door so Laney could exit the room first.

In the kitchen, Laney asked, "Chinese, Italian, Blimpie, chicken? What shall we order?"

"You don't have anything we can make here? That way, we don't have to waste too much time."

"To be honest, I really don't have much to eat here. I haven't gone shopping in a while," Laney said, looking a bit puzzled. Why was Scott in such a rush to get this over with? Maybe it bothered him to be cleaning out his sister's room. He probably said he would help to be nice.

"I could go for some beef and broccoli," Scott finally answered.

"Chinese it is." Laney got the menu out of the cabinet drawer. "What kind of rice would you like?"

"White rice with an egg roll, please," Scott said, taking a seat at the kitchen table.

After three rings, someone answered. "Hello, Delicious China Town, how can I help you?"

"Hi," Laney began. "I would like to place an order to be delivered. Can I get a beef and broccoli combo with white rice and an egg roll, a sesame chicken combo with pork fried rice, and a large container of Chinese iced tea? Can I get that delivered to 77 Lake View Drive, apartment #4. How long would that take? Thank you." She hung up the phone. "Half-hour, they said."

Laney knocked on the door and asked if he was o.kay. Scott opened the bathroom door with a smile. "Yeah, as good as can be." They walked back to Sandra's room together. "So where are you moving to, anyway?"

"I'm moving back home for a while, you know, where I can get my head together and try to focus on the future," Laney responded, then quickly changed the subject. "How about we put the radio on, you know, to give us some kind of motivation?"

Scott suggested they wait till after the food came so they could hear the bell ring, which it did moments later. Scott handed Laney a twenty-dollar bill and said, "It's on me." Laney ran downstairs to get the food while Scott went to the kitchen for forks, napkins, and cups. He seemed to remember where everything was from the last time he was there. About two years ago, Sandra had gotten a teacher of the year award, and Laney had thrown her a small get-together to celebrate.

Shortly after that party, Scott had done some traveling with his work. He never knew where he was heading or when he would return. He really didn't have time to stop in and say hi. Laney figured that was living life in the fast lane.

During lunch, they talked about when they were kids and the traveling Scott had done. Time was slipping away, Laney thought. It felt like they had been sitting there for about ten minutes, but when she looked at a clock, it had been forty-five minutes. Laney cleared the table and Scott followed her back to Sandra's room.

3

After two hours of non-stop cleaning, one side of the room was completely cleared away*nd*. Laney was ready to tackle Sandra's desk, which was cluttered with junk—mostly papers, a few pens, and of course a few empty water bottles. Laney picked up one of the water bottles and found a picture underneath that was half-covered by a piece of crumpled paper. The picture's lower left corner was wrinkled and a bit torn. The photo was of a golden-blonde-haired guy with clear, water-blue eyes. He was wearing a black blazer jacket with a white t-shirt underneath, faded blue jeans, and white plain sneakers. Behind him was a black 2009 Chevy Malibu with leather interior and mirrored windows.

Sandra had been holding this picture when Laney found her face down on the desk. Laney shut her eyes to visualize the memory better. The picture was in one hand, but what the hell was in the other? Laney played the whole thing back in her head. She had walked in Sandra's room after knocking a few times. Sandra had her head down on the desk, the picture in one hand and an envelope in the other. *Was it an envelope*? Laney wondered. She had only seen a glimpse of it. When Laney couldn't wake her friend, she had panicked. She screamed Sandra's name and shook her harder and harder. Nothing happened. Laney had grabbed her cell from her back pocket and called 911.

The ambulance arrived quickly and the EMTs attended to their work immediately. When Laney saw one EMT's face, she knew her friend was gone. They laid Sandra on the stretcher and took her away. Her death was labeled as a fatal heart attack, so there was no need for an autopsy. Laney had one of the doctors at the hospital call Scott to let him know what had happened. Laney had been too shaken up to do it.

Laney was startled by the sound of the radio as Scott tried to find a station. Rummaging through the things on Sandra's desk, she came across an envelope that also had a wrinkled corner. *This has to be it*, she thought. The envelope had no return address. Laney tucked the envelope under her shirt and walked toward the door. "I'll be right back," she said over her shoulder.

She rushed to the bathroom, then slammed and locked the door as if she were hiding from an intruder. Making herself comfortable on the lid of the toilet, she pulled the envelope out from under shirt. As she neatly pulled out the contents of the envelope, she could hear her heart beating loudly. *What did this contain, and why had Sandra been holding it?* Laney unfolded the pages and began to read:

Dear Sandra,

There is no easy way to say this, but I need to tell you. As you know, I've been trying to get closer to you these past few months. You dazzled me from the first time I laid eyes on you. Your amazing smile had me mesmerized, and the way the light sparkled in your eyes was the light that guided my life. With the first kiss, I went weak in the knees.

Over the months, I've showed you my love in so many ways and never asked for anything in return. Still, after giving you all my love, I felt you didn't feel the same. If you loved me, why couldn't you just tell me, show me, anything? In the beginning, I'm sure there were some feelings, but as time went on, I realized that maybe I am not the one for you. I've told you I wanted to marry you and start a family with you. How can you marry someone and spend forever with them if they can't even be honest with themselves, let alone someone else? I know your feelings should be expressed when they're truly meant to be said. Then again, sometimes they need to be heard as well.

Back to my point. I never really knew how you saw me. Did you care for me at all? I guess after a while, I started to question why I was with you. The more I questioned, the more I had doubts and pulled away.

Sandra, I know this is hard for you, just please understand that I never meant for things to turn out as they did. It just happened. It seems like the more you closed yourself off from me, the more open I became toward someone else. I want to be with someone who wants to be with me and maybe have kids someday. I have to follow what my heart tells me, and someday you'll follow yours.

I have to be honest with you, Sandra. I know a letter isn't the way this should be said, but I can't tell you face to face. So please forgive me. For a little while now, when I told you I was working and couldn't see you, I was meeting up with someone else. After you told me what you had done, I figured we were done right then a there, but I couldn't let go that easily. However, it became easier as the days went on. Next thing I knew, I was falling for someone else, who was also falling for me. Things are going good between us, and we are seeing a lot more of each other. I'm sure you know where this letter is going. This will be the last time you hear from me, and I wish you the best of luck for the next person you meet.

Just promise me that you'll always keep your head held high and live for tomorrow with no regrets for yesterday. Don't ever let another tell you that you're not good enough for them. They won't be good enough for you. Know that I will never forget you, and through all of this, I hope you never forget me. You'll always have a place in my heart.

Love always,

Brad Clark

Laney wiped the tears that had fallen before putting the letter back into its envelope. She was more confused than ever before. *Who the hell was Brad Clark, and why didn't I know about him? Why would Sandra keep this from me? What did she do to make him do this to her?* All these questions came to Laney at once. She had to know the truth, solve the mystery. Most of all, Laney wanted to know why Sandra kept this a secret. Laney needed to find the answers, but how? Where would she even begin to search for the answers?

Laney tucked the envelope back under her shirt and ran cold water in the sink. She splashed her face, hoping to get rid of the redness in her eyes. As she dried her face, her mind raced.

Walking back into Sandra's room, Laney had a puzzled look on her face until she was startled by the sound of Scott's voice. "Hey, there you are. I finished the closet. Tell me what you think."

"It looks good to me." Laney looked at her watch. "Scott, would you mind if we call it quits for today? I have a pounding headache and need to lie down." She put her hand on her head as if it was really hurting.

"Sure, not a problem. I'll check on you later to see how you are feeling. If you're up to it, maybe we can finish tomorrow afternoon." Scott walked to the front door of the apartment.

She quickly locked the door after Scott had left and rushed back to Sandra's room. She made it her mission to find out the answers to all her questions. There had to be something in this room that had the answers, something, anything that could help Laney. She didn't care if it took all night, she was going to solve this mystery.

Entering Sandra's room, she didn't waste any time. She pulled everything apart. Although she wasn't sure exactly what it was she was looking for, she tore through everything. She ripped open the neatly piled bags and dumped the contents on the floor. Sandra's desk was next. Papers fell to the floor as Laney rummaged through, looking for whatever she could use.

She turned desk drawers upside-down onto the floor. Once the entire desk was emptied out, the floor looked worse then it did before she and Scott had gone into the room to clean. Laney was on all fours, going through the pile of papers she had created. While picking up each piece of paper, she noticed something in the corner of her eye, something purple wedged between the desk and wall. Laney paused a moment before moving the wooden desk away from the wall.

"Oh, shit! Bingo!" Laney said out loud, though she was alone. It was the answer to all her questions. It was a diary. Sandra's diary! Laney never knew Sandra had even kept a diary. Laney was bound to find out who Brad Clark was and what really had happened to her friend. After reading that letter from Brad, Laney questioned the fatal heart attack they had written on her death certificate.

Grabbing the diary, Laney rushed out of the mess she created in Sandra's room. She made herself comfortable on the living room sofa. It would take her a long while to read through this diary. She turned on the end table lamp, took the throw blanket off the back of the sofa, and began to read.

4

January 3, 2008

Dear Diary,

I've met the man I have been dreaming about for as long as I can remember. He is exactly the way I pictured he would be, from his head down to his feet. And here I thought it was hopeless for dreams to come true. A few days back, I was standing in front of the library when a gust of wind nearly knocked me over. I was carrying a lot of books when I lost my balance. I tripped over a crack in the sidewalk, and down I went. Books went flying as I landed. I was so embarrassed, I rushed to my knees and started to pick up my books, which needed to be returned to the library.

As I was picking up the books, there he was bending down to help me. My heart stopped, I couldn't breathe, and my body went weak. He looked at me with a smile I'll never forget. His golden-blonde hair was neatly cut and matched his dazzling blue eyes. They reminded me of the clear blue water, of an ocean that meets the white sandy shoreline. His words were softly spoken, "Are you okay?"

Oh, my god, I couldn't talk. I was spaced out. All I could do was nod my head up and down. How embarrassing was this? He helped me to my feet and took the books from me. We both walked into the library without saying anything. Once I returned the books, we found a spot in a quiet corner where we could talk for a brief moment. Well, a brief moment became a few hours.

For some reason, I felt so comfortable with this stranger. I opened up to him rather quickly, as he did to me. We let the time go by as we listened and learned about one another. While he was talking, I couldn't help it, I really wasn't paying attention to what he was saying. My thoughts were perverted. Who could blame me? He was hot, and I wanted him badly. I wanted his juicy lips on mine as I watched them move when he spoke. I fantasized his hands exploring my body as my heart beat faster.

What the hell was happening here? I need to calm down and brace myself. This had never happened to me before, not that I can recall anyway. *Just breathe and relax,* I told myself. After a few moments I came back to reality as he stood up and asked what my plans for tomorrow were. Thank god I didn't have class. "Nothing at the moment," I managed to say.

Grabbing my hand to kiss it, "Would you mind meeting me here tomorrow then?"

How could I object? Hell yeah, I'd meet him.

But I was calm with my response. "Absolutely," I managed to say while my body trembled. I stood up to watch him leave, and I went weak at the knees. I wasn't quite sure what had just happened, but I loved every minute of it.

Unlike any other man, I needed this one. My body cried out to have him touch me, probably in a way I'd never been touched before. I wanted him all to myself. I can't spend one more day not knowing him. I am so hoping he will kiss me tomorrow. I know I just met him and all, but hell, I don't care. I fantasized for the rest of the day as to how his lips felt, and how it would be to have his naked body against mine. Who knows, what if he was thinking about me in the same sense I was thinking of him? One can dream, can't they?

I've been counting the hours until I can see him again as I play back everything from this morning. It still doesn't seem real to me. I'm just waiting for him to turn around and say, "Smile, you're on *Candid Camera*." That would be my luck.

January 4, 2008

Dear Diary,

Well, I went to the library as planned. I got there early as hell; I didn't want to miss him. What if I was late and he left thinking I stood him up? Yes, I know I'm retarded. I can't help it. This guy drives me crazy. Anyway, my heart was beating so fast. I was so nervous, I felt my breakfast getting ready to backfire.

At any moment, this guy who I have been fantasizing about all night long was is going to be there. The funny part about this whole thing is I never even thought to ask his name. Here I was drooling over some guy I don't even know. He could be a psychopath for all I knew. And yet, who would have thought I'd react as I did over him? Damn, he isn't just some guy; he is *the* guy. I had to focus on our conversation today and remember to ask his name.

After an hour, I decided to pick a book off of the return shelf to pass the time. He never really said what time he'd be there, plus I didn't want to look desperate. I was just turning to page three when I heard an unforgettable voice.

"Are you enjoying the book?"

I glanced up at him. "Nothing wrong with a good book here and there." He smiled at me. His smile was deeper and more welcoming then the day before, and his eyes were amazingly hypnotizing. I put out my hand for a proper introduction. "My name is Sandra."

He put his hand out as well. "It's nice to meet you, Sandra. I'm Brad Clark."

Brad Clark, a name I'll never forget. He was so casual as he said his name. His words were softly spoken, and his eyes sparkled when he talked. *Is it getting hot in here, or is it just me,* I thought.

He leaned in and asked, "Would you like to have a cup of coffee with me?"

Would I? Hell yeah! I wanted to say. I swallowed the lump in my throat that was beginning to form.

"I could use a cup of coffee right about now," I said with a sweet and innocent smile.

We went to this little corner coffee shop two blocks from the library. As we walked, he grabbed my hand and held it. I felt my body heat up in an instant. I couldn't help myself. I had to find out how his lips felt. We came to a brick building at the corner. I pushed Brad up against it, without any warning, and kissed him. It was like fireworks on the Fourth of July. His lips were juicy and soft, as I imagined they would be. I wanted to suck on them forever. His mouth was warm and inviting. He slowly moved his tongue as he grabbed me to kiss me back. For a few moments our tongues intertwined.

My knees started shaking as they went weak. My heart was pounding so hard I thought it was going to come out of my chest. This was the first time I had ever felt this way. I didn't know what I was feeling or what to expect. Whatever it was, it was definitely real.

The kiss, like everything else, ended. We continued our walk to the coffee shop. "Well, that was exciting," Brad said, smiling at me. After entering the coffee shop and sitting down, I told him that I hadn't stopped thinking about him since he left me yesterday. He looked at me as if to say, "Me, too," but he didn't say it. It's all good though. He was hot, and I was sitting next to him at a coffee shop.

I'd never really noticed this corner coffee shop before. Every time I walked by, it was dark inside and looked closed. But that was the idea. It was one of those places where you could go if you needed a break from life without being noticed. When Brad and I went in, there were only two other people sitting in separate booths and three workers. I could definitely be discreet in this place. Even if someone you knew came in, he or she wouldn't be able to notice you. The lights were dim like candlelight, and the booths were round with high backs to promote privacy.

So even though Brad and I were hugging and kissing like two teenagers under the high school bleachers, no one could see us. We were like a match made in heaven. He kissed me the way I wanted to be kissed, and I kissed him back the way he wanted me to. He suggested we go back to his place to get out of this wicked cold. Let's face it—there is only so much coffee you can drink. I agreed without hesitation. I was shaking on the inside, as he led the way to his black 2009 Chevy Malibu.

I didn't know what to expect when we got to his house. Was he expecting sex? After all, I didn't really know him. Maybe he was just being nice, or maybe he wanted someone to talk to. Whatever he wanted, I think I was up for it—including sex. I couldn't help it; that's all I was thinking about. It's not like I asked to go to his place. This was all his idea.

Once we entered his one-bedroom penthouse apartment, he scooped me up in his arms and put his warm, soft lips on mine. My body was heating up, and I was so aroused just by his kiss. I wanted to push things further, but I didn't want to seem like that's all I was there for. My knees started to shake when he unzipped my coat. Within seconds, my coat was off and Brad was leading me towards the couch. *This is it*, I thought. *It's going to happen on the couch. Where's the romance in that? Maybe I was right, maybe Brad just sees me as a piece of ass. An easy piece, at that.*

Though the thought of being easy lingered in my mind, I still needed this man. I still wanted him to make love to me long and hard, or short and sweet. Either way, I wanted his penis inside me. I wanted him to push up in me as far as he could go. I wanted him to make me scream and beg him for more.

My thoughts were interrupted when Brad stopped kissing me. I didn't want him to stop. It was my fault. Brad stopped to take off his coat. I was too caught up in my own world and didn't realize he still had his coat on.

Brad walked over to his surround-sound stereo, asking me if I wanted a drink. He put on some slow jazz and walked into the kitchen. He came back with two glasses of lemonade. *Lemonade!* Who the hell would want lemonade now? Hell, I wanted Brad-ade. I wanted to drink every last drop of him. Now that would be yummy.

We spent the rest of the afternoon talking and sipping lemonade. I listened to Brad talk while I fantasizing about him naked. I admit I am the weak one here.

I lost track of time. Two hours had passed, and I had to leave. God knows I didn't want to. "I hate to leave, but I must go. I'm meeting a friend for lunch. Would you like to have coffee another time?" I asked as I put my coat on.

"Absolutely," he said, grabbing my hand as if to stop me from leaving him. His lips were soft and full of motion as he kissed me good-bye.

It's weird—you think you really know yourself until a hot, dreamy guy comes along, and bam! You forget everything. Then again, what am I saying? I've never felt the way I do when I'm with Brad. I feel like I am dreaming when I am with him, then I wake up when I have to go back to my real life.

It was a good twelve-block walk from Brad's apartment to mine. The wind was blowing bad, and the bitter cold was getting colder. Trash was getting blown all over the streets, and people were rushing and trying to hold on to their hats. I didn't care. I was on cloud nine. I got home with a quickness, and my body was still overheated from being at Brad's house. I wanted to see him tomorrow, but he said he had a few things to do, so he didn't want to make a promise he couldn't keep. At least we exchanged cell numbers. This means he wants to talk to me again. If it's possible to see me, he said he would call me. I hope he does call so I can hear the deep, sexy voice he has.

5

*L*aney adjusted the pillow behind her back before reading more of the diary. She was very puzzled by all this. Although she wanted to be mad at Sandra for not mentioning any of this to her, she was hurt at the way she had to find out. It was very upsetting for Laney not to know of the strong feelings Sandra had for this Brad guy. Laney didn't know if she should keep reading or not. This diary contained Sandra's most personal, private, inner thoughts, and Laney felt like she was invading that. Then again, if she didn't finish reading, she'd never learn why things ended as they did, or most of all who Brad Clark was. Laney must keep reading all the way to the very end.

What if Sandra left the diary there because she wanted Laney to find out everything? If Sandra truly wanted everything to stay a secret, she would have burned the diary or something, Laney thought. She made herself comfortable again and began to read. Laney hoped Sandra would forgive her for invading her privacy.

January 8, 2008

Dear Diary,

Damn, it's been five days since I had heard from Brad. Why do guys do that to woman? They say they'll call and never do. Oh yeah—because they have a penis, and we allow ourselves to be used by them. If he didn't want to see me, he could have just told me. Of course, that would be too easy. All men suck, and if he does ever call, I should be like, oh, now you know who I am. Maybe it's for the best, because at least I still have my dignity.

As much as I wanted to, I couldn't stay mad. I sat there day after day fantasizing about what could have happened that day at Brad's house. I can't help the way I feel. I haven't even slept with the guy yet, and I can feel the way it would be if he did touch me.

With the thoughts of him holding me and kissing me, I feel the warmth of his touch as it surrounds me with lust. I can feel his body pulsating as it caresses the beating of my heart. The thoughts of him stagger in my mind and capture my emotions. My need for him is now the air I breathe and the strength of my weakness. With his eyes, what does he see? With his heart, what does he feel? With his mind, what does he think? The thoughts of him touch my soul, while the touch of his soft lips lingers on my body, as I pulse to climax. He caresses my body with his gentle touch as he explores with his tongue deep into my soul. Why can't I see, why can't I feel the one I need? He is only a dream, a fantasy, just a thought.

While I was deeply thinking about Brad, he finally texted me. He said he's free tomorrow, if I want to meet up with him. You would think I would ask why he hasn't called, but I didn't. I just want to see him. Hell, I didn't even care that he didn't call. Hopefully, tomorrow we go a bit further then kissing. I won't initiate anything; if he pursues it, I just won't object.

Am I really falling for this guy? I'm having all these thoughts and feelings. Am I falling in love with him? Do I tell Brad how I am feeling? He may think I'm obsessed and really never call me back. Should I at least tell him I want his body? Oh god, what is wrong with me?

January 9,2008

Dear Diary,

My heart is still pounding from the experience I just had with Brad. Amazing is the only way I can sum it up. Oh, man, where do I begin? For starters, he picked me up a block away from my house. That is where I told him to meet me. He had a dozen red roses in the front seat waiting for me. How sweet was that? He helped me into his car and kissed my hand before closing the door. He made me feel special when he did that.

Once he had gotten into the driver's side, he said he had another surprise for me, but I had to wait until we reached his place. I wondered what that could be. Reaching his apartment, my heart beat fast. Helping me out of the car, he gently kissed my lips. He looked deep into my eyes as if to say something, then he looked away and led me to his penthouse apartment. On the way up to his floor, we held hands and childishly bumped into each other.

Brad has a really good personality. I think that is what draws me to him. He isn't uptight like just about everyone else I've dated. He loves to smile and makes me laugh every time we're together. Not to mention he is very romantic and has a sensitive side.

Finally, we reached his apartment door. He took my coat and asked me to wait in the hall for a few minutes. I figured he needed to hide his other girl. I need to give him more credit than that. Maybe he had to finish up the surprise he had for me. That was Brad though, always full of surprises. I found it to be one of his romantic traits.

After about five minutes, he came and asked me to close my eyes. Suspense is what I hate the most about surprises. Before closing my eyes, I saw the anticipation in Brad's face as he grabbed my hand. He led me into his apartment and directed me right where he wanted me. I felt his soft lips on mine before he told me to open my eyes. Once I did, it was a surprise well worth the wait in the hallway.

The living room was lit by candlelight, and there was a silk blanket spread out on the floor with a few pillows on it. On the blanket was dinner for two. *How sweet*, I thought, *a dinner picnic in the winter.* There was a bottle of sparkling white champagne in an ice bucket next to the blanket. I was amazed by this seducing sight. I knew that Brad's intentions involved more than just dinner tonight. Judging by the way this was well thought out, we were definitely on the same page.

We sat close together on the sprawled out pillows as we ate. We fed each other little nibbles here and there, with some kissing in between. Dinner went on for a long while. Every second passing seemed like time was at a standstill. It seems like the world stops rotating on its axis when we are together.

Brad cleaned up the dishes and food from the floor after refusing my help. Once he sat down again, he leaned in and gently kissed me. Damn, this guy drives me wild. Not even kissing me for two seconds, and my body was getting all hot and bothered. I had to have him immediately. As he was kissing me, I felt him get a little forceful in laying me down on the floor, which I didn't object to at all. I went easily with the flow.

His kisses became deeper and deeper, while his masculine hands started to explore my pulsating body. He started with my face, then wrapped both hands around my neck and nibbled on my lower lip. My bodily fluids were ready to explode. From there, he sucked on my neck like a vampire biting its prey. I let out a slight moan to let him know I wanted more, much more.

My body was trembling when his hand cupped my breast and massaged around my erected nipple. I almost came in my pants. It was coming, and it was coming fast. I couldn't stand it anymore. I pulled his shirt off and started to bite his neck like a bloodhound eating a raw steak. Oh god, this man was so sexy. The scent of his cologne aroused me more. I wanted to scream, "Fuck me!" but I regained control of myself before doing so. My thoughts were interrupted when I felt his fingers slide into my vagina. That's it! I lost all self control and came all over his fingers. I was like a volcano waiting to erupt. My moaning got louder and my breathing got heavier. Within seconds, my pants were off and his hard-ass cock was inside of my lava-flowing vagina. I was moaning louder than before. I wanted deeper and harder. It was pure pleasure, and I didn't want it to stop.

While penetrating my vagina, he held me in his arms and looked deep into my eyes. I gazed back, thinking to myself, *So this is what making love feels like.* He was so in tune with me and what I wanted from him, it was like our hearts beat the same rhythm. We had our first sexual moment, and it was slow and passionate and meaningful. It was nothing like wham bam, thank you ma'am. The more I said, "Don't stop," the deeper inside me Brad's penis went. Seconds later, I felt the quick pull, and there was hot cum oozing down my stomach. My sexual moment was over. He then kissed me and wiped the cum off my stomach. We laid there for a bit, both of us breathing like we had run three miles. I was so comfortable lying in his arms, I didn't want to get up and get dressed. But as you know, all good things must come to an end.

Brad dropped me off one block away from my actual block. I didn't want to take the chance of anyone seeing me getting out of his car in front of my house. The truth is, I didn't want to be questioned about who Brad was. We kissed one last time before I got out of his car. I'll spend the rest of the night replaying the whole evening in my head, detail by detail, until I fall asleep.

6

January 14, 2008

Dear Diary,

Well, it's been five days since I've seen Brad. I can't stop thinking about him. Day and night, and in my dreams, it's Brad, Brad, Brad. What is a girl to do? He is so amazing; who could blame me for constantly thinking of him? We have been talking 24-7 since that magical night. I feel like a kid with my first crush. I get butterflies in my stomach and an ear to ear smile appears on my face when my phone lets me know a text message has gone through. It is unbelievable how fast I am developing feelings for this guy. I'm falling hard. I just hope I'm not setting myself up to be let down. I'm not going to let that thought dampen my mood. Brad is like a dream, a wonderful dream that is coming true for me. I always dreamed of meeting a man like Brad, but to actually have it happen is heaven.

The wait to see him is a struggle, I'm not

going to lie. I don't want to sound like one of those annoying, clingy girls who are like, "Why can't I see you, and why didn't you call me in ten minutes?" Way too much drama for me. Still, it would be nice to see him every day. It's hard for me to understand why I miss him so much after only seeing him a few times.

The sound of the phone made Laney jump. She closed the diary and got up to answer it. "Who the hell can be calling me now?" she said aloud. "Hello?" Laney answered in a semi-cranky voice.

"Hey, Lane, it's me, Scott. I just wanted to call and see how you are. You seemed a bit weirded out earlier."

With a shy smile, she said "Yeah, Scott, I'm okay. It's really nice of you to check on me."

"So what are you up to?" he asked, hoping to strike up a conversation with Laney.

"I'm just making myself a cup of tea, relaxing, getting ready to read a good book." Good book indeed. The clock on the stove read 8:30 PM already. Time flies when you're not interested in it. "I'll call you tomorrow. We can set up a time to finish cleaning that room. Thanks again for being concerned. Bye," she said and hung up.

She felt bad for hanging up on him, but she had a lot more reading to do. This wasn't the type of book where you would read a bit here or there each night before going to sleep. This diary had to be finished tonight. At least, that was Laney's goal.

Walking back to the living room, Laney thought

that maybe she should have told Scott about his sister's diary. Then again, what would he do? Come running over here to read his sister's private thoughts? I guess some things are best not said.

Laney had already drank half her tea before returning to the couch. She made herself nice and cozy, as if she were settling down for a long winter's nap. She adjusted the tableside lamp to make better reading light and picked up where she had left off. Laney turned the T.V. on so it wouldn't seem like she was alone, and maybe she wouldn't get startled if the phone rang again. By the time she started to read again, it was already nine.

January 16, 2008

Dear Diary,

I finally got to see Brad after, like, seven days. He said he got held up with work. I was skeptical at first, but I didn't really know him well enough to be questioning what he does when he isn't with me. I was just happy as hell to see him again. He said he wanted to see me as well. I still feel like I am dreaming, especially since he is so sweet and romantic. We went to this really nice Italian restaurant. The place had low, dimmed lights, and a violinist played at the tables. It was really amazing.

After we had finished eating, but before dessert, Brad took my hand and led me to the dance floor. He held me tight as we swayed along as if we were the only two dancing in the place. He smelled so good. Looking into my eyes, he finally spoke. "Feels like a fairytale, doesn't it?" Then he kissed me in a way that made me weak at the knees. This was definitely the guy I had been looking for. He was my dream come true. The dance ended, and before we sat back down, he kissed my hand and thanked me for giving him the honor. It may have been a line of bullshit, but who cares? I was falling for it.

We ended the night by going back to his place to watch a movie. Yeah, like that happened. The movie was on but we, however, made our own adult movie on his black leather sofa. This time, it was a bit rougher and hotter and sexier then the time before. We were all over each other like pigs rolling in the mud. It was definitely a night to remember. Late, after we had finished and I was getting dressed, Brad asked if I would go away with him one weekend. Um, hello? I just met you, like, yesterday, and you want to take me away to some exotic place where no one will hear me scream as you murder me? Yeah, it didn't happen like that. I, like a dumb ass, said, "Yes, I'll go."

Moments later, we were in his car on our way to my house. Well, the block before my house. As I got out, he had warned me ahead of time that he wouldn't be able to see me for a few days again. He had a lot of work to do with his job, and this time he had to go to China and finish up some stuff. Like that didn't make me question what his job was, not to mention how much time it took away from his personal life.

Still, it's none of my business to ask such

personal questions. When this subject came up, he said he was in sales and left it at that. *But what does he sell?* I wondered. Maybe I'll bring it up the next time we have dinner. After all, I was sleeping with him every chance I could get. I should know some personal things about him.

As soon as I reached my apartment stairs, a text came through on my cell. It read: *I miss you. Love, Brad.* Aw, how sweet. He misses me already. It's only been, like, two minutes since I had gotten out of his car. Wait a minute! Did I read this right? *Love, Brad.* Was he trying to tell me something? Maybe he was falling for me the way I was falling for him. You never know.

After I let my emotions get the best of me, I came back to reality and decided not to make a big deal out of this. It could just be a normal reaction to write love on everything. Plus I had more important things, like his job, to wonder about. I just hope he doesn't blow it out of proportion as to why I want to know. What if he does tell me, and I realize I was better off not knowing? What the hell was wrong with me? Oh, god, I need help. Why do I even care what his job is?

January 24, 2008

Dear Diary,

Yup, you guessed it. It's been a few days since I've seen Brad. I know he said he was going to be in China, but this long? Was it like this every time he went there? I hope not. Even though we haven't seen each other, our phone chats are getting pretty intense. The more I talk to him, the more I am falling for him.

Pathetic, I know, but I got it bad. I almost forgot—he sent me flowers today. He sent them to my job, which I'm glad he did, and not to my house. I was delighted to get them and of course surprised. It was really sweet of him. Not just any flowers, but white roses, in an old-fashioned vase with little hand-carvedd flowers. The card read: *Hello, my darling. I miss you with every passing minute of every day we are apart. These are to cheer you up since I can't be there with you for another week. Don't worry, dear, I'll make it up to you. Love, Brad.*

There it was, the "L" word again. He probably writes that when he signs his name. It was really nice of him to send the flowers, I thought. At least he pays attention to me when we talk. I had told him that white roses were my favorite flowers when we first met. I left the flowers in my office. I could have just told Laney they were from a secret admirer, but I didn't want to lie to her. Some things are best unknown. I'm sure it's better this way.

7

January 30, 2008

Dear Diary,

I finally got to see Brad today. Even though it was only for lunch, it was worth it. I took a half day today because I didn't know how long Brad had before he needed to return to work. He's working locally for some time, so I'm taking all the time with him I can get before he has to go away again.

You better believe my heart is still pounding from the experience I had this afternoon. Never in my life would I have thought of doing this. Brad and I met at this small luncheonette just outside of town. After we ate, Brad gave me a necklace that he had gotten during his stay in China. It was breathtaking. It was a diamond-studded heart attached to a thin rope chain. He put it on my neck as he kissed me and told me how much he had missed me.

This guy was definitely a dream, a fairytale,

an imaginary vision, and here he was having lunch with me. I must be the luckiest girl in the world, at least I thought so—and that is how he made me feel. I excused myself from the table to use the restroom. Surprisingly, no one was in there, or so I thought. Walking into one of the stalls, I was startled when a tap on my shoulder made me jump. It was Brad. Before I could say anything, his lips were on mine like glue on paper.

His lips were warm, and his mouth was inviting. His hands went full force over my body, grabbing and caressing everything in their path. We both nearly fell over as he pushed me into the stall, locked the door, picked me up, and pinned me against the stall wall. How convenient I was wearing a skirt today. Unzipping his jeans to expose the hardest erected penis I've seen, he ripped my thong off. The strength this guy had was unbelievable. I felt like I was in a porn movie. It was awesome.

I let out a moan as his erect penis forced its way into my tight, wet vagina. He was pounding me like a construction worker with a concrete power drill. He was so powerful, holding me in one hand, the other one gripping the top on the bathroom stall. Thank god no one came in. Even though we were in the stall, the sound of Brad pounding me was enough to give anyone a mental picture of what was going on. Brad pounded harder the more I moaned. *If he keeps this up, the stalls are going to fall down like dominos. How funny would that be?* Funny and humiliating at the same time. And then, oh hell no, he did it. Brad had ejaculated his load inside me. It filled my vagina like stuffing fills a turkey.

Okay, now I know I should have said something right then and there, but I didn't. Brad should have asked if it was okay to cum in me. He didn't know if I was on the pill or not, that's number one. Number two, he knew he wasn't wearing a condom. Why would he do that intentionally? He looked at me with a satisfied smile and kissed me. After fixing himself, he left the bathroom. Hell, I didn't even know if he would be out there when I came out. I looked in the mirror. My face was all flustered, and my legs were swollen in the middle. I put cold water on my face, hoping it would wash the I-just-had-sex look off my face.

I had all these emotional thoughts going through my head, not to mention I felt kind of used. I think what bothered me most was that for the first time, Brad had made me feel like I was just a piece of ass. Maybe I was just being paranoid. I took one more glimpse in the mirror and exited the public restroom.

I sat back down at the table with this "I can't believe I just did that" look, and Brad was still there. He looked at me with those hypnotizing eyes and asked me if I was okay. "Yes, I'm okay."

Brad looked at his watch and seemed a bit disappointed when he announced he had to be back at work in thirty minutes. He paid the bill and apologized for rushing out the door. He wasn't even gone for five minutes before I got a text from him. He apologized again and said he would make it up to me. He didn't have to, I told him. I understood why he had to go. I wasn't upset.

I spent the rest of the afternoon playing the rewind button in my brain. I repeated every small detail as it happened. I was so dazed and confused about everything that was going on. I think I was just confused at the whole fact that I really didn't know how Brad saw me. *Am I just a booty call? Am I his girlfriend? Does he really want me to be in his future?* All these thoughts were hitting me at once. Then again, it's really too soon to know what I am. Even though it seems like forever since we met, it has only been a few weeks. I'll let faith handle this one.

I hope I get to see him soon. It seems like the more we do see each other, the more time he spends traveling with work. Then our time becomes more distant in between. I'm lucky if I get to see him three times a month. I kind of know what I would be getting into if this became serious between us. The long days of endless dreams, wishing he were with me, endless nights of loneliness. Not to mention the suspense about the kind of work he does.

Maybe I'll tell him first how I feel before he says the "L" word to me again. This way he'll know that I feel the same, and then he will be around more. At least, that is what I am hoping, but I doubt it will happen that way. For all I know, it may backfire on me and he may not speak to me anymore. That would be my luck.

Brad also told me that he would be busy with work for a few days, plus another trip to China.

Of course, a guy's way of saying disappointing news is by a text message. Once I had gotten that message, I called him. I needed a bit more insight into what his job was. It was definitely more than just sales. His tone when he answered, if not his words, said, "Don't ever call me. It's not safe. I'll call you." Whatever that was about, I have no clue. I just got right to the point. No need to delay what I wanted to know. He was quiet for about two minutes before a long "huh." Then another pause. Finally, he answered my question. What the hell was the big secret in telling me? All he does is buy companies that are going bankrupt, then break them up into pieces and sell them off to bigger companies. A one-man company could end up in, like, eight pieces with eight different people owning it. That's crazy, but the way Brad put it was, "It's just business." Nonetheless, a lot of his buildings are located in China. Wow, what a shocker there.

At least now that I know that, maybe my mind will be at ease. I now understand Brad Clark and why so much of his time is taken. It was as simple as one, two, three. And Brad didn't seem mad that I had questioned him. Which was good, because now I can be open with him the next time something is bothering me.

February 1, 2008

Dear Diary,

Today was a good day. It was the kind of day

you wish would happen more often in life. Even though I hadn't seen Brad in a few days, he was still sweet over the phone. He spoke words that are unforgettable. In fact, I can still hear his voice, clear as day. He told me that he was falling in love with me. His feelings were getting stronger and stronger with each passing day. He knew this was happening fast, but he had no control over his feelings. He felt like he had known me his whole life and that I had been put on this earth to be with him. He didn't want to live another day without knowing me.

My heart melted like ice on a hot, sunny day. No one has ever said anything like that to me. This was my chance to tell Brad how I felt, that I did love him and that I also was falling in love. Instead, "That was really sweet, Brad," came out. I choked again and couldn't get the words to come out. I had the perfect moment to tell Brad how I feel, and I didn't. He must think I am stupid. A grown woman who can't even say I love you. At that moment, I thought Brad was going to be like, "Well, do you have anything you want to say to me?" But he didn't, nor was he mad. I'm really surprised that he was so calm, in fact. When you open your heart like that to someone, you expect the same in return. It may not be the same words, but something, right? Maybe he just figures that when I am ready to tell him how I feel, it will be true and straight from my heart. I mean it now, I know deep in my heart I do, but for some reason I have a hard time telling Brad.

I was thrilled about what Brad said to me;

however, I am bummed out because he also said he wasn't sure when he could see me. It may be a week or two. I guess it is understandable, but I am still disappointed. In a way, it's a good thing. This way, he does what he has to, and I can focus on my students. I haven't even prepared them for mid-terms, which are next month. I've been so into Brad that I've been blind to everything else. Although I miss him like crazy, we both need to focus on reality when we are apart.

8

February 5, 2008

Dear Diary,

Brad finally texted me after a few days of no contact. He was held up and couldn't call me, or see me, for that matter. His trip has taken longer than planned. He is in China again. I wonder if he would ever invite me to go with him? He can't be working 24-7 when he is there. He must get some time off, I would think.

Although I understood, I was still upset. What could I say about it? Please quit your job, I am lonely without you? I doubt that would go over well. He would definitely think I am obsessed with him. It would be nice to see him more often. You know what they say, though—business is business.

He had asked me to go away with him for Valentine's weekend. Of course I will. One whole weekend, just me and him. I couldn't wait. Interesting—he never did mention where we were going. I said yes to go away with no clue where I had said yes to go. Yeah, I'm obsessed. The only thing he said was that he had a wonderful surprise, which, coming from Brad, usually was a wonderful surprise. You better believe I am counting the days to the love-making fest.

I don't have a clue what it is about Brad, but that man makes my body quiver, just by his looking at me. It's really hard to describe. I have never felt this way before in my whole life. I am like a reborn virgin. I think that Valentine's weekend will be the perfect time for me to tell Brad how I feel about him. I will tell him that I love him, and that he is my world. When I look into his eyes, my world makes sense, and when he kisses me, he is giving me life. Hopefully, I don't get all choked up like usual. He needs to know how I feel before he doesn't think I feel anything at all.

February 9, 2008

Dear Diary,

I just had an amazing time with Brad. I was getting out of work and walking across the parking lot to catch the bus. It was way too cold out for me to walk. I got halfway through the parking lot when I heard a whistle. It was Brad. He was leaning up against his car with a boyish look to him. I couldn't help it, a big smile lit up my face as I greeted him. He opened the passenger door so I could get in. Once he was in the car, he leaned over toward me and kissed my cheek.

"I hope you are hungry" was the only thing he

said to me. Not even a "Hello" or "Do you want to have dinner?" Nothing like that. *How bizarre,* I thought, *and mysterious.* I like it. I was in suspense to know where we were going to eat. But, you know Brad, it was another surprise. I tried to find out, but it was no use. I was told to sit back and enjoy the scenery, so I did.

I liked having a guy that knew what he wanted and what he was doing. Brad had a sense of direction and knew where he was heading in any situation. I couldn't be bothered with the "What do you want? Whatever you want. Where do you want to go? Well, where do *you* want to go?" That shit aggravates me to no end. Thank god Brad wasn't like that. It makes what we have more interesting, whatever it is we have. Not to mention my favorite thing was that I never knew what to expect with Brad.

After an hour and a half of driving to god knows where, I asked if we were almost there. I had to pee like a race horse. Good thing I always carry a puzzle book to do; otherwise, I would have been bored out of my skull. I didn't act like I was bored. Brad answered, "Almost there." Where the heck were we eating, west bumblefuck? Who the hell drives this far for food? Not me, that's for sure. Damn, I needed a bathroom a.s.a.p. My bladder was going to explode. I would of gone beforehand if I'd known we were driving to the end of the world. I didn't want to sound ungrateful, but this drive had better be worth it.

After another twenty minutes, we finally arrived at our destination as the sun was setting.

We ended up at a little jazz spot called Shondra's. It was a classic, old-fashioned restaurant located high up on a mountaintop. The view as I got out of the car was breathtaking, one I'll never forget. The dusky sky overlaid the ocean with a purple skyline, as if it were a Bob Ross painting. It was beautiful. I didn't know what town I was in, nor had I ever heard of this place. I'm just glad I got to experience it with Brad. It was definitely worth the trip, if only for the view.

The food was like nothing I had ever tasted, and the music played was like a scene from a movie. Everything fit together as it was supposed to. This surprise was the number one of all the surprises he had ever showed me. I told him I felt bad that he had driven all this way to romance me. Then again that was Brad's thing with surprises, always going to the extreme.

As the night progressed, so did my courage in telling Brad how I felt about him. After all, anyone who goes through this much trouble was entitled to hear how a person feels about them. My heart wanted to burst out "I love you!" but my mind, however, was on a different level. I was stuck again. Instead of me saying what I wanted to, "Thank you for an unforgettable evening" came out.

The whole drive back, I was trying to figure out why I had such a hard time telling Brad how I felt. I get the urge to say it, and then boom! Just like that it's gone. He held me with one arm as he drove, the sound of soft jazz coming from the car stereo. Maybe if I don't think about saying what I want to and get myself all worked into a nervous wreck, maybe, just maybe, I will be able to tell Brad that I love him. Not to mention feeling safe and secure in his arms.

I must have fallen asleep on the way home, because getting back to town only seemed like a half-hour drive. I awoke with the touch of Brad's lips on my forehead. Just like that, my fairytale was over, and I was back home. We had a short, sweet kiss, and the night was over. As I walked into my apartment, I thought about going away with him in a few days. Am I ready for all this? I mean, going away with someone I don't know. I wanted to get some advice on this matter, and the best person for it is my one true friend, but Brad is something I keep to myself for some reason. Not that Laney would object or criticize me. I just feel it's best unknown at the moment.

9

February 12, 2008

Dear Diary,

I am kind of annoyed at the moment. I hadn't seen or heard from Brad since our romantic dinner, and then finally, today, he demands that I meet him this evening at the café. Um, hello? "How are you?" would have been the right way to address me. How about "Sorry" and a reason for not knowing me for those few days? That would have been logical. I knew he wasn't working. Then you are just going to be like, "Meet me here," and I'm supposed to because you say so? Yeah, let me know how that works, pal.

I told him I couldn't, even though I was happy as hell to hear from him. I wanted to see how he would react. Not that I said it in those words, anyhow. I simply said I wasn't feeling well, which I really hadn't been this morning.

Brad was understanding about me not meeting him and was really sweet towards me as my day went on. He was like, "Are you okay, baby? You need me to bring you anything?" You know, stuff like that. He even sent me flowers with "Get well" balloons, as if I had major surgery. You would think that now would be a good time to tell Laney about him, considering the flowers were sent to my house. Nope, I just said they were from a co-worker and hid the card. If I tell her about Brad, then he wouldn't be my secret. He wouldn't be all mine if someone else knew about us. I know how retarded that sounds, but that's what I think.

However, on a good note, I will see Brad in two days for our romantic Valentine's get away. I will get to be with him for two nights and three full days. Now, that was a dream come true. I'm not really sure as to where we are going, but who cares? I am going with my McDreamy, and that's all I needed to know. Plus, Brad wouldn't give me a hint, so I just gave up in asking. I just hope he isn't expecting too much from me. I've never really gone away with someone after only meeting them weeks earlier.

I can't stop thinking about all the sex we're going to have. We will lay on the beach all day, if there is a beach, make love under the stars, have breakfast in bed. Yup, this was definitely going to be a romantic getaway. The more I think about it, the more I can't wait to go, even if it's just to relax and unwind. Actually, the main reason is because since the first time we made love, each time is better, so I can only imagine what this trip will be like. Hell, I even looked up a few new sexual positions on line. Pathetic, I know, but I don't want him to get bored with me.

We did talk about anal intercourse once before, but I am so not ready for all that now. Maybe somewhere down the road. The long, long road of, say, about twenty years. It figures he would have to mention it. I was like, "Um, I'd have to think about it." What is it with men and anal sex? Every guy I had ever been with wanted to try that nonsense. Not this chick, sorry. I'll just change the subject every time he mentions it and see how long that lasts before I have to come up with another excuse. One day, I'm sure I'll love him enough to do it.

Laney closed the diary and got off the couch. Making her way into the kitchen, she was stunned by the secrets her best friend had kept from her. She made another cup of tea, as she thought over and over about this whole mystery thing. The stove clock said 9:45. Scott popped into Laney's head on her way back to the couch. She had a secret as well. She was head over heels for Scott, and although she had plenty of opportunities to tell him, she never did. She always acted calm and cool whenever Scott was around. It was hard, but she didn't want to seem like the annoying kid-sister type with a big crush—even though she was, and she was still crushing over him. She wondered if he ever thought about it.

Laney shook her head as if to shake away the thought and sat back down. Picking up the diary again, she wondered what was to become of this

Brad guy. Was he really all that Sandra made him out to be? There was only one way to find out. Laney knew there was no going around it—she had to finish the diary tonight, no matter how long it took her.

February 17, 2008

Dear Diary,

Amazing, amazing, amazing, is the only thing I can say about the romantic getaway. Brad was truly amazing. He really went all out for this trip. We went to this little island just off the coast of Mexico. The sand was white, the water was crystal blue, and the best part was that we were the only two people on the island. It was deserted this time of year. There was a small cabin with a fireplace and a hot tub. Palm trees with coconuts surrounded the cabins. I felt like I was on an episode of *Survivor* when Brad said we had to look for some wood. These three days went by with a quickness, and yet every moment felt like forever. I don't even know what to say about our love making. Amazing.

When we had first arrived on the island, we tied the speed boat up to a wooden dock. I couldn't believe at how hot it was—in February, at that. Good thing Brad told me to pack for hot and cold weather.

The place we stayed looked like a rundown shack. Although we had to do some clean up, it was a really nice place. The inside didn't look as bad as the outside did. However, the bedroom was perfect. It had an aroma of jasmine, and the bed was covered with red and white rose petals. There was a pink bottle of champagne on ice with two glasses on the night stand. There was soft jazz music playing, and the room's only light came from three pillar candles on the dresser. Brad grabbed me from behind and walked me toward the bed.

My heart raced and my body quivered with the touch of his hands massaging my breast. My bodily fluids were already starting to flow. My clothes were off, and he laid me on top of the rose petals. My nipples were harder than they had ever been. Soon, Brad was sucking on them like an infant trying to get milk from its dried-up mother.

I let out a pleasurable moan when Brad buried his face between my legs. I was completely out of control, and cum was everywhere as he licked his way to my soul. He did this for a long while. I was trembling everywhere, especially when he caressed my inner thighs while licking me. After moments of me begging that I wanted him, Brad inserted his erect penis deep inside me. The walls of my vagina were pulsating hard and rapidly. My cum was like hot, liquid lava escaping the rumbling volcano.

Looking into my eyes, he began to move slower and slower. Then the words "I love you" escaped his lips. I just returned the look and kissed him. *Here we go again,* I thought. I do love him, I just can't bring myself to tell him. I know he was expecting to hear it in return, although he never mentioned it. It was the way he acted afterward that led me to believe he wanted me to say it. He just pulled out of me without even finishing. For some reason, I wasn't feeling well at all. I rushed into the bathroom and threw up. *How romantic,* I thought. When I came out of the bathroom, Brad was already dressed.

We ate dinner that night on the beach. The sky was lit by millions of twinkling stars. I don't think I had ever seen a night sky like that. Brad, of course, made a fantastic dinner for two. We set up a small table on the sand and lit a few lanterns for light. I couldn't help but wonder what was to happen after dinner. We mainly talked during dinner. Well I did, anyway; Brad mostly listened.

He was upset, I'm sure, about the whole "L" word and what happened before. I just hoped he would let it go and not be like this all weekend. Just because I don't say it doesn't mean I'm not feeling it. I don't understand why this is so complicated. It shouldn't be, after all. It is just a four-letter word.

After dinner, we walked on the beach in the moonlight for about a half-mile around the island. We were holding hands and bumping into each other playfully. I didn't even care if we made love that night or not. It was still a romantic evening. It was a bit colder than when we first arrived. The thought crossed my mind of a nighttime swim, but I was too cold to suggest it.

Making our way back to the cabin, Brad asked what was on my mind. I said that the whole night had been like a dream come true. At that moment, he pulled me towards him and kissed me underneath the starlit sky. I wish I was as calm as the water looked. The current was slowly moving to where the reflections of the moon and stars were at a standstill. It reminded me of a peaceful, still August night. I would have taken a picture, but I had forgotten my camera, and so had Brad. Nor did he try taking any pictures on his cell, which was with him 24-7.

The weekend passed so quickly, it felt like I blinked my eyes and it was over and back to reality. Brad was leaving for China again. At least this time he told me that he wouldn't have cell service in the area he had to go. It would be a waste to call him or text him, and he would inform me of his return. This was the topic of conversation on the way home.

I had him drop me off in front of the school, figuring it was easier. He kissed me like he was kissing his mother on the cheek. Then he said, "I'll call you when I get back." God only knows how long it will be this time. In a way, I was upset about not talking to Brad, but on the other hand, I really wasn't feeling too well. Maybe it's the flu or some kind of stomach virus. I was nauseous the whole way home. I have to make a doctor's appointment, just in case it is the flu. Hopefully it isn't. I can't afford to miss any more work.

10

February 22, 2008

Dear Diary,

What a waste of time. I went to the doctor's office today, and he told me I have allergies. I never knew that allergies could make you puke. But hey, I have a teaching degree, not a medical one, so whatever. He took blood and told me to call him back in a few days. If I had known that, I would have taken some allergy medicine and gone to work instead of taking yet another personal day. Oh well, what can you do?

Still no call from Brad. I know it's only been a few days, but come on now. This is annoying. Too bad I didn't meet Brad a few years back. Then I would be past the whole "I love you" stage, and it would be okay for me to tell everyone. He would be mine. Well, one can dream, can't they? I think the real thing that is bothering me is his job. I know we talked about it, but was China the only country in the world where he could buy property?

I've never heard him mention anywhere else that he visits for work. It seems like it's his second home. Come to think of it, he is there more than anywhere else.

February 26, 2008

Dear Diary,

Oh, my god! I am sure glad I went to the doctor. It turns out that I don't have allergies after all. I'm pregnant. Yup, I said it. Pregnant with a capitol P. I'm just a few weeks along. Oh my god, what am I going to do? I can't have a kid. At least, not now. I'm just learning how to take care of myself. How do I take care of a baby? I don't even know how to change a diaper. How could I be so stupid and get myself into a situation like this? What the fuck was wrong with me?

When the doctor came into the room to tell me the results of my blood work, he said, "Well, it's not allergies. Congratulations. You're pregnant."

I had this stupid look on my face and was like, "Who is pregnant?"

"You are," the doc said with an angelic look on his face.

"The hell I am," I said.

The doctor could tell by my reaction that this wasn't a good thing. He gave me some ideas on how to deal with this type of situation. The first choice he recommended was adoption. How would I be able to carry a baby for nine months, give birth to it, and then give it a quick glance and hand it over to a complete stranger? How would I be able to go on with my life knowing that a child exists in this world, and that I am the one who gave it life? I would always wonder what he or she would look like, if they were loved and being taken care of; if they ever knew the truth about me, and the fact that I gave him or her up. Would I ever want to search for this child and be part of their life?

Second, there was the option of keeping the baby and waiting for motherhood to come to me. I could take classes that would teach me how to change diapers and make bottles, and how to nurture a baby. That would be great—a teacher taking classes on being a mother. A single mother at that. I have no guarantees that Brad would even want this baby—or even want me after I give him this wonderful news.

Third, I could have an abortion, basically killing what was starting to grow inside me. How do these people go through life using this as a method of birth control? It's okay if we get pregnant, I'll just get an abortion, they think. I'm not sure I could go through with it without any regrets. Then again, if I do decide to go this way, it would be a one-time thing. If that means no sex again ever, then so be it. What would Brad say about that? How would I even say it? "Hi, how are you? Oh, by the way I aborted your child."

What would he say about any of this? Now that question was popping in and out of my mind while I was finishing up with the doctor, who said he would give me some time to think my decision over and to get back to him. Once I decided, he would set me up with the right people to make my decision possible.

That was the start of my day. Then I was kind of pissed, since I still haven't heard from Brad since we had gone away. Are you kidding me? This is getting ridiculous. I'm the one who is always sitting here and waiting, hoping he will come around and see me for what I really am and not a Playboy bunny. It is really starting to get to me. If he does decide to call me on his return, I should play hard to get and see exactly where I stand. Maybe then I'll get somewhere with him.

Brad and I had never talked about having kids, or getting married, or anything that involved the future. Actually, most of our conversations really had no meaning at all, now that I think of it. Who knows, maybe I can change that by letting him be part of the decision I have to make. I wish I knew just what to do at any given moment; then I wouldn't be where I'm at today. I don't take rejection too well, so I think it's best if I just make the choice on my own. I have the fear that he will be like, "It's not mine," or "Is it mine?" Like I'm a whore and sleeping with different guys while being with him. You know how men can be.

Whatever way I do choose to go, I need to do it soon. I'm on the borderline for getting an abortion. Once I reach a certain point in this pregnancy, it will be too late for that option. I told the doctor I didn't want to know any specific details, such as when my due date would be, or the time I conceived, or anything else that would make it any harder than it already is for me to decide. I think I am definitely on my own for this decision-making process.

Everything is so messed up right now, and it is all my fault. How could I be so careless knowing this could happen? You see shit like this all the time in the world, and you always say: "That's not going to be me." And now look, it is me. I gather that the only solution to this situation would be to get the abortion and not tell anyone. Maybe this way I'll feel like it really never happened. At least no one knows I am pregnant, nor can you tell I am yet. If I go through with it, no one will ever know. I'll give it a few more days to think it over and see if that is the way I want to go or not.

March 4, 2008

Dear Diary,

I'm not sure at the moment as to how I should be feeling. Should I be pissed and angry and go into a psycho screaming phase, or should I be upset at the fact I still haven't heard from Brad? This is the longest we have gone without talking, and let me tell you, it sucks. Although it has made it easier for me come to a decision about this pregnancy. I decided to go through with the abortion. It seems like the best way to go, with less regret. Even more so since Brad doesn't talk to me anymore. I don't even know if he has returned from China yet.

It is amazing how within a few days, my life went from having everything figured out and doing what I want to make a good life for myself to being more confused than ever, not knowing what to do anymore, losing sleep over everything that's been happening, and above all being a pregnant slut who is going for an abortion in a few days. I don't get it. And the man who once said he loved me hasn't returned any of my calls since that last time I saw him, Valentine's Day weekend.

He probably moved on to his next victim in his sex scandal on how to make woman feel like they are his everything and then never talk to them again. Why couldn't he just tell me he was done with me and didn't want to see me anymore? Why do men feel as though women can see into the future and know why they stop talking to us? If that is the case, fine with me, but an explanation would have been appreciated.

//

March 12, 2008

Dear Diary,

Today was the worst day I have ever had. When I would fantasize about my future, getting an abortion wasn't part of it. It's done and over with. I know I made the right choice, yet I feel like shit. I feel like a bad person. I didn't feel like this beforehand, when I made this decision. I didn't think it would hurt this bad, either. I should have kept it and made it work somehow. I'm sure I would have had help from Laney and Scott if I needed it. Once it was over and I had recovered from the anesthesia, a cloud of regret came over me that still hasn't lifted. I made the wrong choice.

Who cares if Brad didn't want to be part of his kid's life? I would have found a way to get through it. A lot of woman are single parents, and they make it through. Now it's too late. I did it. I aborted my baby. I'll never feel it kick inside me or know if it was a boy or a girl. I'll never get to look into those eyes and know I made the right decision by keeping this little precious angel. I'll never hear the word mamma or hear its first laugh or hear it cry. I'll never know what it would be like to have a baby by a man I am in love with. How could I do such a horrible thing? I made a terrible mistake, and now I have to go through the rest of my life paying for it.

Every time I see a little baby in a carriage at the park, I will think of my aborted baby. Or when my friends have their kids around me, it will bring back the memory of the abortion and how I'll never get to see my baby grow. I don't even know how to move on from this. I don't think you really get over something like this. As for Brad, I think it's time I got over him.

Laney closed the diary and started to cry. She cupped her face with her hands and bent down into her lap. This was the first time she had let it all out since Sandra died. Everyone kept asking if she was okay because no one had seen her cry. She was fine—at least, that is what she said to everyone. She would let out is a tear here and there. Now, she couldn't turn them off. They were pouring out, and she had no control over it. She cried at the thought of losing her best friend, the thought of Sandra having to make such a big decision on her own, and most of all she cried about the pain Sandra had gone through, which Laney had known nothing about. It was like Sandra had this whole other life that only she and Brad existed in.

Laney jumped to her feet when the phone rang in the kitchen. *Who the hell could be calling me at this time of night,* she wondered. "Hello," Laney answered in a stern voice.

"Hey, Laney. It's me, Scott. I um, I was thinking about you and wanted to see if you were okay. You sounded a bit nerve-wracked earlier when I called."

With hesitation, Laney managed to say, "I did, didn't I? Sorry. I have a lot on my mind. You know, with the move and all. Seriously though, I'm okay."

"Would you like to have lunch with me tomorrow afternoon? Afterward, I can help you finish up what needs to be done, if you'd like."

She couldn't help but smile. "Thanks, that would be nice. I would very much like that. It was really sweet of you to call. I appreciate it. Night, Scott. I'll call you in the morning to set a time to meet. Bye." Laney hung up the phone. She had to get to the bottom of this immediately.

March 20, 2008

Dear Diary,

Finally, I heard from Brad today. He texted me in the morning, saying good morning and how are you and all that stuff. I wanted to be mad, but surprisingly I wasn't. I was casual and my heart was pounding hard. It made me smile from ear to ear when I saw his text. He told me he missed me and that he wanted me to meet him for dinner. I should have told him to fuck off; instead, I said, "Of course I will." I couldn't help it; I missed him too much. I had to see him.

It's not his fault; after all, he did just get back from China. Here I am getting mad at the guy for doing his job. Truth is, I really don't know what he was doing. I just have to have faith that he was really working. At that moment, I didn't even care what he did. I just wanted to be with him.

After my excited moment had passed, I wondered if I should tell Brad about the abortion or not. I really don't want to bother him with all that drama now, especially since we haven't seen each other in, like, a month. I don't want to damper the moment. I'll tell him next time. It's not like he knew I was pregnant to begin with, so why tell him the horrible thing I have done? Some things are best left unsaid. Besides, what is done is done.

March 25, 2008

Dear Diary,

Now I know how Cinderella felt. I just had a romantic evening with Brad. What can I say? The man makes me glow. His words were so romantic and unforgettable. We met by the school where I teach. As soon as he arrived, I felt butterflies rising up in my stomach. *Here we go again,* I thought. Brad had gotten out of his car with open arms and scooped me up. He hugged me for a while as he lifted me an inch off the ground. It felt so wonderful to be in his arms again. Before he kissed me, he looked into my eyes and said that he missed me. "Not a day passed where I didn't thought about you. I felt like something was missing from me when I couldn't hear your voice." He put me down and then hugged me again.

It may have been a bullshit line, but I fell for it. He opened the passenger door for me, and I sat on a small black box on the seat. It was a small jewelry box, I'm guessing. My heart was in my throat, like any other woman's would be when given a small jewelry box.

"Is this for me?" I asked when Brad got into the car.

He answered with a little-boy smile, "Why of course it is, darling."

I opened it, trying not to look nervous. Thank god it wasn't what I thought it would be. It was a diamond pendant on a white gold chain. All I could say, after catching my breath, was "Oh, Brad, it's ... it's beautiful. I love it." I took the delicate piece of jewelry out of its box and handed it to Brad so he could put it on me. He gave me a gentle kiss before he pulled away from the front of the school. He held my hand the whole way to a beach in the middle of nowhere. I was going to say something, but I didn't. I know from past experiences that Brad's surprises are well worth the wait.

I'll never forget the way the beach looked that night. The sky was dark, with a purplish tint to it. The moon was big and full, and its reflection glistened on the water's surface. On the shoreline, the slowly moving water met the soft sand. A candlelight dinner was set for two on a quilted blanket spread out beneath the place settings, and there were pillows for extra comfort. This must have taken a lot of planning.

Although the food was delicious, we rushed through it. Brad had another surprise and wanted to hurry and pack everything up. I was hoping to make love on the beach, but I knew that was out of the question when we headed for the car. Once we were in the car, Brad asked if I was in a rush to go home. Hell no, I wasn't. I answered more calmly then that. I was happy because I had thought Brad was ending our date early. He just had something else planned, that's all.

He made a right turn onto a familiar block. We were going back to his place. *Thank you lord*, I thought. We found a parking spot in front of his building, and this time I let myself out of his car. A misty rain began started in the chilled night air. My heart beat faster and faster. I knew what was going to happen in his apartment.

He let me enter his apartment first, then he spun me around and kissed me. Gazing into my eyes, he then said these remarkable words I will never forget: "I love you so much, I carry you in my spirit everywhere I go. You're in my thoughts day and night. I pray for you more then I pray for myself. I think we should take our relationship one more step. I don't want to spend one more day not knowing you."

Holy crap, I almost came in my pants. His words were softly spoken and followed by another kiss. So many things were going through my head at that time, I couldn't even think on what to say in return. I just returned the kiss as passionately as I could. My heart was racing, my juices were flowing, I had to have him right then and there. So I did.

He started to fondle me, following my lead. Both of us were breathing heavily. Clothes were falling on to the floor around us. Then Brad picked me up and carried me into the bedroom. As soon as Brad laid me on the bed, he was on top. He was caressing my body with his soft, gentle, masculine hands. Cum was flowing out of me like a waterfall. I couldn't take it anymore. I had to be in control of this operation. I flipped him over like we were on a wrestling mat in the gymnasium of the high school. I was now on top, demanding the moves Brad originally intended on doing. I pinned him down as I slid his hard, erect penis into my hot, moist, welcoming vagina.

I toyed with him for a bit. I would insert his penis deep inside me, then pull all the way out. After a few times of doing this, he was begging me to ride him. The harder I pushed my hips down on him, the louder he moaned. "Oh baby, please, don't stop. Yeah, that's the way I like it!" I leaned back, his penis still inside me, and massaged his balls. Brad grabbed me by the arms and flipped me over. My legs were wrapped around his waist, and his hands had my hips lifted off the bed as he penetrated me. I moaned with pleasure. This went on for hours, the two of us trying to dominate each other.

And then, just like that, it was over. The ringing

of his cell had taken over his erect penis, and down it went. Who the fuck was calling him at 3:30 in the morning? At first, Brad acted like he didn't care who was calling. If that was the case, then why did he look at the caller I.D when moving the phone from night stand to dresser? It was an amazing night, so I decided not to make an issue of it. Without any words, Brad kissed me good-night after getting comfortable in bed again. He pulled me toward him to lay in his arms, and that is how we fell asleep.

The next morning, I was awoken by the smell of Belgian waffles with maple syrup, sausage links, and Italian roasted coffee brewing in the kitchen. Damn, not only was Brad a charmer and really good in bed, he was a chef as well. Then again, this was Brad's way of doing things. He never took short cuts. He always went to extremes for me. It was sweet and really thoughtful of him to do so.

Brad quickly showered and left for work. On the way out the door, he told me to stay as long as I'd like. How nice it would be to wake up every morning to Brad's face and kiss those lips every night before closing my eyes. Now that would be heaven.

12

April 17, 2008

Dear Diary,

For the past few weeks, Brad has been truly amazing. Even though I haven't seen him since the last time we had dinner and I slept over, he has been terrific. I have heard from him every day since then, sending texts non-stop during the day and talking for hours on the phone at night. I've noticed a major change in him. His "I love you" and the things he wanted to do to me when he saw me were a bit overwhelming, but I didn't mind. In fact, I was as happy as ever.

During our late-night chats, we would have phone sex. To me, that was just a big old tease, but Brad seemed to be into it. So as long as it was for Brad, I was all for it. Not to mention the pictures we were sending from phone to phone. Shit, *Hustler* magazine was PG-13 compared to our pictures. It was fun, though. I felt like a young girl just starting to experience the jungles of nature.

I've noticed that the longer Brad stays away, the closer he becomes to me. He is starting to open up and is making me feel like more than just an easy piece of meat sold in a butcher store. Although I don't hear from him the whole time he's away, he seems to want more when he comes home, which is good for me. It's the moment I have been waiting for. Maybe there is a future for us after all.

He asked to take me to dinner, which of course I accepted. I couldn't wait to see him. He said he would be arriving in two days, and he would pick me up as soon as he left the airport. I wish it was now. Two whole days can take forever. I need to just keep myself busy, and hopefully time will fly. The suspense of where we are going doesn't help either. It is never the same thing twice with Brad. Plus, he puts in a lot of thought when it comes to me. I am definitely going to tell him about my strong feelings for him. He is the air I breathe and the soul of my body. I can't bear to live without him. Which brings me back to my thought on the abortion—do I tell Brad or not? It's only right that he know the truth. Eventually, I do need to tell him. I'm sure he will understand. That is the way Brad is, very understanding.

Then again, we never really did discuss the whole kid subject and wanting them. I guess some things are just best as is. If it isn't broke, don't fix it, unless it is absolutely necessary. Still, what's done is done. Who knows, maybe one day children and marriage will be a topic of conversation, but not today. We live different lives, and babies don't fit in right now. I know Brad will feel the same way. It's only been a few months; I am not even sure we are a couple yet. I'll just take it one day at a time and see what happens. One thing I know is that I can't wait too much longer about telling Brad how I feel. He may think I don't feel the same and move on. I can't let that happen.

April 19, 2008

Dear Diary,

I finally got to see the love of my life. God, he looked so damn delicious. He picked me up as planned, and instead of going someplace to eat, he took me back to his place and ordered some Chinese food. After we ate, we made ourselves comfortable in each other's arms and began watching a movie. Like that lasted long. Within moments, we were kissing hot and heaviy. Hands started wandering and clothes started falling. This was my moment, and I took control.

I made Brad sit on a chair in the corner of his living room. I then straddled him with my back against his chest. I leaned back on him and put my arms up around his neck. Brad wrapped one arm around my waist and caressed my exposed breast with the other. His lips felt so warm on the back of my neck. My juices were flowing like the day Mt. Saint Helens erupted. My heart was racing and my breathing was hard. I moved up and down, clenching my clitoris as I went up on Brads erect penis. I rode him nice and slow for a while. As I massaged his balls, Brad's moans got louder and louder. Then without warning, Brad pushed me off him and bent me over the coffee table. He was fucking me from behind. Grabbing my waist, he pulled me towards him as his balls smacked against my ass. He was ramming me hard. Hell, I didn't mind. I was loving it.

Then, holy shit, I felt a full nine-inch erect penis in my asshole. The shock of my life! Brad had taken my anal virginity. Oh god, this was painful. You think you would warn someone before shoving nine inches of penis in someone's ass. I was numb from the waist down, and I was praying Brad would cum soon. I swallowed my pride and held my dignity while Brad performed anal sex. He was only at it for, like, three or four minutes when I felt my back fill with his hot steamy cum. God must have heard my prayer. At least Brad wiped his cum off me.

My anus was throbbing when I walked afterwards. Brad had asked me to stay over, but all I could think about was a hot shower, so I said no to staying over. He was okay with it and offered to drive me home. I told him to rest, and that I would text him letting him know I got home safe. I just needed some time to think about what happened and what to do about it. Should I say something to him? Should I be pissed that he would do such a thing? All these thoughts were going through my head. I didn't even bother to text Brad when I got home.

April 24, 2008

Dear Diary,

I had just spent a quiet evening with Brad. Surprisingly, we didn't make love. Hell, we didn't even caress each other. At first, I thought he was mad at me for not staying over the last time. Then I figured that it is okay to just cuddle and hold each other as well. It's nice to know that what we have just isn't about sex. We rented a teary movie from Blockbuster and ordered in from the Italian restaurant on the corner of Brad's block. It was pretty nice, I have to say. I was lying on Brad's chest as he held me in his arms. Then he kissed my head and whispered those three words again, "I love you."

Here we go again, I thought. I almost had the words out, but instead, "I know" came out. I just couldn't get the words out. This was starting to be an ongoing thing. Why was it so hard for me to tell him how I felt? That question had haunted me for weeks now. I turned to kiss him, then we finished the movie in silence, holding each other.

It is amazing how three little words have so much meaning and can change your life forever. It can be scary and exciting all at the same time. It seems like Brad is saying it more and more to me lately. Is he trying to get me to say it in return, or is he just trying to let me know he means it? Either way, it is stressful. It's not that I don't love him; I just don't think I am ready to say it. I hope Brad understands that, when I eventually do say it, it will be worth the wait to hear it. It will be very meaningful then. I am not going to plan on saying it either anymore. When it happens, it happens.

May 1, 2008

Dear Diary,

It has been seven days since I have spoken to Brad. He won't return any of my texts, and when I try to call, it rings once then the voicemail picks up. What the hell? Is he avoiding me? If that is the case, why can't he just tell me? Maybe he's mad at me for not returning his words of love. Although it wasn't said, what if it did bother him that I never opened up to him when he did to me? He could've just told me he was upset when I was at his house. I would've explained why it is difficult to say it to him. But no, men just think women are supposed to know what they are feeling. I must have missed that class in high school. I thought Brad would be understanding about all this; I guess I was wrong.

Even though I am upset, I still miss him like crazy. I need Brad in my life. He is everything I have ever wanted in a man, and I waited so long for someone like this to come along. I am going to keep trying to call him until he at least tells me why he is doing this. He never mentioned going back to China, so I know he isn't there. I just wish he would tell me so I am not wondering day after day.

Then again, this is how Brad works. We see each other one night and don't talk for a few days.

It does get annoying after a while. If I thought it was worth it to say something, I would. I don't think it will do any good, though. No matter how mad I say I am at Brad, once I hear from him, I am not mad anymore. As long as I do hear from him, I am happy. It is actually a relief that he isn't getting rid of me so quickly. I just hope he comes around soon and lets me know what you would call this thing between us. If it is a relationship, then he needs to be more appreciative of my feelings. It is fine we can't see each other every day, but at least let me know instead of not telling me anything at all.

May 10, 2008

Dear Diary,

This was the longest we had gone without talking. And then I got a text message from Brad. I got happy without even reading the message. Just knowing it was from him was exciting enough. He was like, hi. Are you kidding me? No explanation—nothing. Then he asked me to meet him for dinner tomorrow night. How could I say no? I just couldn't wait to see him. The thought crossed my mind that I am really desperate. This guy doesn't talk to me for weeks, and now he says "Meet me," and I go running. I wonder how long this will last. Maybe he thinks I am not worthy of an explanation. If it were someone other than Brad, I would have been like, "Screw you, buddy," after the first time. I was never into anyone the way I am with Brad. He completes me.

We talked through text for hours on end. We laughed, we talked about sex, and then out of nowhere, he brings up kids. That was a shocker. We had never talked about anything along those lines. Our conversation turned serious. He told me how he sees me in his future, and how he wants to have kids. He never mentioned marriage, though. Kids were the topic of conversation for the majority of our chat. I kept trying to change the subject, but it wasn't working. The more he mentioned it, the guiltier I felt. I aborted his baby, and he doesn't even know. I had to tell him. It was the right thing to do, no matter what the outcome may be. Shortly after that, I had gone on the pill. He was making it a habit to cum in me, and I didn't want to be in that situation again. I think I would want to be married first before having a baby.

I'm just so scared about telling Brad what I have done. I figure I'll do it after dinner tomorrow. This is the moment I've dreaded for the longest time. I just wish there were an easier way to tell him. For weeks, I wondered what his reaction would be if I told him. I guess I'll find out tomorrow night. If I didn't have to tell him, I probably wouldn't. It's better to find out sooner than later, I think.

Then again, who knows? He only just started to mention kids. He may understand why I did what I did. He has to know where I am coming from and the situation I was in. After all, it's my body; don't I have say? The final decision should be mine. I figure I'll say something when he is driving me home. This way, we are alone, and I won't be too far from my house if he throws me out of the car. I doubt he will do that, but you never know.

13

May 11, 2008

Dear Diary,

Oh god, I wish I could say this night was worth seeing Brad, but I can't. It started out like any other spent with him. He picked me up at our usual spot, on the corner half a block away from my house. He was leaning up against his Chevy Malibu when I approached him. He held open the passenger door so I could get in. He brushed my cheek as I got in and shut the door. My heart was beating faster and faster. I had the taste of vomit in my mouth and a lump in my throat. I was disgusted by the secret that haunted me. And now, it was all about to be revealed.

I was quiet as Brad pulled away from the curb. We ended up going to a small Greek restaurant on the other side of town. During dinner, I mostly listened to Brad and how he would make father of the year. Brad talked more than he usually does. In fact, I don't even think he noticed how quiet I was. Even if I did want to talk, I would not have been able to get a word in.

Brad went from how much he missed me, to being a father, to eventually getting married someday, and back to fatherhood again. I just wanted to scream, "Jesus, shut up about this whole baby thing already!" Instead, I sat there trying to hold my food down. Before the check arrived, I told him I wasn't feeling well and wanted to make it an early night. Brad was cool with that and agreed to take me home after he had paid the check.

As soon as we had gotten in the car, he started talking about baby names. If it is a girl this, and if it is a boy that. That was all I could handle. "Stop the car!" I yelled and got out as soon as he did. He stopped in front of a small city park a few blocks from my house. I had taken more than I could handle and let out my frustration. For the first time since I've known Brad, he had this puzzled, confused look on his face. He followed me out of the car and kept pace quickly behind me.

I led Brad to a bench, where I sat to catch my breath. I sat there for a few moments, staring at a fully grown spruce tree until he finally broke the silence. He asked me what was wrong as the tears in my eyes started to form. And so I began to tell Brad the truth about everything that had happened. It came out a lot easier than I had thought it would.

I wasn't looking at him when I started to talk, so he grabbed me by my arms and forced me to look at him. I couldn't hide my tears anymore. "I don't know how to say this to you. It is something that you do need to know. I was pregnant with your baby."

At first, Brad looked delighted, followed by a puzzled look. "What do you mean, was?"

"I found out I was pregnant shortly after we had lunch and did whatever in the bathroom. I hadn't heard from you in weeks, and you weren't responding to any of my texts. Once I received the news from the doctor, I was confused, scared, and helpless all at once. I didn't know what to do. By you not answering any of my calls or anything, I was stuck in a tough situation. I had no one to turn to. An abortion seemed like the right choice at the time. I was running out of time and had to make a choice fast. So without any question, I went and had it done. I'm sorry. There was no contact with you, and I wasn't ready to be a single mother."

I was trying to hold back the tears that were stinging my eyes. I glanced at Brad, who was trying to make sense of what I had just told him. And then, unexpectedly, I saw a look of anger and disgust come over his face. It was a look I will never forget. Then out of nowhere, *slap!*

Within seconds, my right cheek stung. I could feel Brad's handprint becoming a welt on my face. That was something I never imagined I'd have to deal with. Then came the words of hate that will haunt me forever: "You killed my baby without any concern that I may want to father it. Without considering my need for fatherhood. You really are a selfish whore. In fact, I can't bear to look at you anymore." Brad walked away. He took off in his car without even a glance at me.

My knees went weak, and I fell to the bench in a hysterical crying fit. I was crying so hard I could barely breathe. *What have I done*? was the only question that kept repeating over and over in my head. The tears kept falling with no control as my whole world came crashing down in a matter of ten minutes.

Brad is my whole life, and now I have nothing. The more I thought of him not being in my life, the more I cried. Brad was right—how could I do such a selfish thing? It's too late now, I can't change the past. If only I had kept the baby until I was certain Brad didn't want it. He would still be talking to me. Then again, I only had a certain amount of weeks, otherwise I couldn't get the abortion. I just hope he comes to realize that I would lose either way. Have the abortion and lose Brad, or keep the baby and wonder if I was going to end up a single mother on welfare. That wasn't the lifestyle I wanted for my child. That is, when I was ready to have a child. Why can't he understand my point in this situation? I just hope he calms down and talks to me again.

The only thought that boggles my mind now is, do I beg for forgiveness or just let things end as they did? I waited so long for a man like Brad, and I had to go and fuck things up with my selfish acts. Who could blame him for being so mad at me? I would have probably done the same thing if the shoe was on the other foot.

You know what? Fuck that! That still doesn't

give him the right to hit me the way he did. Being mad and yelling is one thing, getting physical is another. Why would I even want to know him after what he had done? I saw a side of Brad I never knew existed, and I do not ever want to see that side again. I'll tell you one thing, I'll never forget the hate in his eyes and the rage in his voice. I know he was pissed, but he didn't have to hit me. Doesn't he know that people make mistakes? It's not like he was there to help me make the right choice, either, so why am I the one taking all the blame?

No matter how much I love Brad, I refuse to stay with a man if he puts his hands on me. I don't deserve to be treated like that, nor will I lower my standards and live with it. If Brad ever decides to talk to me again, this will never happen again. If Brad cannot understand that, well, then he can go fuck himself. Everyone has limits, and this is where I draw the line.

14

L aney paused a moment in reading the diary. She felt terrible for her friend. If only Sandra had come to her. Laney would have been there for Sandra every step of the way. If only Laney knew the pain her friend had held inside her, maybe she could have helped her overcome it. Laney shook her head as sadness filled her heart. If only Sandra had let Laney be part of this secret life she led, maybe everything that had happened in the past few weeks could have been avoided. Now it was too late. Laney reopened the diary and picked up where she left off.

June 8, 2008

Dear Diary,

It had been almost a month since I last heard from Brad. I hadn't tried to contact him, either. He really must have been pissed off. Then, out of the blue, I received a text message from him. He asked if I could meet him for dinner and said that he needed to talk to me. Not that I'm sorry for what I did or anything. He just expects me to run every time he calls, because he knows I will. Of course I agreed to meet him for dinner. He told me when and where, and that was the extent of our conversation. *Great,* I thought, *he is going to break off all ties with me, or maybe he wants to apologize because he feel terrible about what he has done. Here we go again, another night of unanswered questions haunting my brain.*

The good side to all this is that one, Brad finally texted me, and two, I don't have to live with that guilt anymore because Brad knows the truth. You can't imagine the relief I feel about that. Even though I was going crazy not talking to him, I just couldn't give in and call him. Everything happens for a reason; maybe he now knows that I am not going to kiss his ass. Either way, I am just happy I am going to see him in a few days.

He told me to meet him at that small Greek restaurant on the other of town at seven, and that he may be a bit late. He wanted me to go in and get us a table. He said he had to make a small stop along the way. I'm okay with that. If I know Brad, he'll stop at the floral shop to surprise me with flowers. That is really sweet of him.

I am a bit curious to know what it is he wants to talk to me about. Is it good news? Bad news? Great—more questions to keep me baffled for the next few days. Why does everything have to be so hard? He didn't seem angry through his text, so maybe he was missing me. I don't know. I think I am just going to take it one day at a time and see what he has to say.

I tell you one thing, this suspense shit kills me. It must be good news, or even okay news. Why would you ask someone to dinner to give them bad news? You would just meet at the park or a café or anywhere else, I guess. Anyway, I am so excited to see him that I went out and bought this really nice outfit. It is going to blow his mind. At least, that is what I am hoping for.

June 12, 2008

Dear Diary,

Where do I begin to tell you about the evening I just had with Brad? It sure as hell didn't go as I planned. It wasn't the best night I had with him, but it definitely wasn't the worst, either. Let's just say I shouldn't have gone through with it, but I did, like a pathetic loser.

Apparently, a bit late meant that Brad was going to be an hour and fifteen minutes late. He showed up at 8:15. I wonder where he had to go, because he didn't bring flowers or any other gift that would have made him late. So, like a jerk, I sat and waited, sipping water, trying to act casual so no one would notice me. At least this time he did warn me ahead of time that he was going to be late, so I really couldn't get mad at him. He finally showed up with a "hey how are you doing?" smile. It felt like we were old buddies meeting for a drink. He didn't even try and explain why he was so late. *How rude,* I thought, but he did show, so I was happy about that.

Brad took the honor of ordering food and drinks for both of us. As soon as the waiter left, he went straight into it. "I am sorry for reacting as I did. Your words took me by surprise, and my actions took over before I could think about it. I hope you understand that I never intended to hurt you. I know that isn't an excuse for the way I behaved. I just hope you can find it in your heart to one day forgive me. Anyway, I had asked you here tonight to tell you that and hope you accept my apology."

Hell yeah, I forgive you. I didn't say that out loud, though. I was overwhelmed with joy inside. I did say, "Apology accepted." I picked up my glass of champagne. "Here's to a new beginning." Life was good again. I felt like I was able to breathe without hyperventilating. I had Brad back, so nothing else mattered.

Having said that, Brad wasn't the way he usually was with me. All during dinner, I was talking and Brad was texting, saying he was sorry and then asking me to please continue. What the hell was that about? Then he ate his dinner for about three minutes before rushing to the bathroom. He had the nerve to send me a text from the bathroom. It read, "Sorry for leaving the table as I did. I am not feeling well and need to go home. Don't worry; the bill is paid for. Stay, finish your dinner, and feel free to order dessert. Talk to you soon, Brad." Are you fucking kidding me? I waited for over an hour for this guy to leave me in the middle of the restaurant? After a few moments, I calmed down a bit and realized that he must really be sick to do something like that. Then I felt guilty for being mad at him.

I got up and walked out of the restaurant, trying not to look humiliated. I called Brad to see if everything was okay; of course, there was no answer. Did I really think he would answer? I had to text him. No response. Could I really be this stupid and desperate for a guy? How could I put myself through all this hurt and pain? The tears began as I started my journey home. I was twenty blocks from my house and had on Nine West stilettos. I'd feel it in the morning, that's for sure.

Every time Brad had done something like not call me for days, or not show without a text or anything, I never questioned him. But I am not letting this go. Next time I talk to him, I am going to demand answers. Why he couldn't come back to the table and tell me he was sick and we had to leave? I would have been fine with that.

June 15, 2008

Dear Diary,

It has been seven days since I last saw or heard from Brad. I know I promised myself I wasn't going to text him, but I am worried about him. What if he is really sick, and here I am being selfish again by getting mad at him? I wish he would tell me what is really going on so I can understand a bit better. Of course, he didn't answer text or phone.

What I don't understand is why did he apologize if he had no intention of talking to me? God, why does this have to be so damn difficult? I understand people get busy or sick, but let someone know instead of ignoring them. That's how it should be. I guess men prefer the guessing game instead. I am going to wait a few more days before I text him again. If no response, then I am going to his house. He'll have to talk to me if I am standing right in front of him, right?

June 20, 2008

Dear Diary,

Finally, I heard from Brad. I texted him, "Are you okay?" earlier today before going to his house. Hours later, he responded. He said he was okay. I suggested that we meet for coffee or something. He didn't say it directly, but I got the hint. He was at work and too busy to see me. He would let me know when he had time for me. I didn't know I was such an inconvenience for him. Fine. Whatever. He'll call me when he is free. I guess I just sit and wait around for him to call. At first, I thought he was blowing me off, but about an hour later, he texted me again, suggesting we meet sometime next week. I said okay, and that was the extent of our conversation. My guess was that he was going back to China when he said he would call me when he was free. That was his usual line when he went there.

Why do I love this man so much? This is something I ask myself every minute of every day.

Even after everything we have been through, or everything he has put me through, I still love him. He is the blood that flows through every vein in my body. I am so lost without him, and I do not wish to live my life without him in it. But it seems like he is slipping away from me. I know he needs some space, but how much?

I understand people deal with things in their own subtle way, but treating me like this should not be a form of dealing. He should be happy that I told him about the abortion. Most girls would get pregnant on purpose to cover up their secret. I swallowed my pride and told him so I wouldn't feel guilty, and somehow it backfired and I'm the one being punished. Not once, but twice. I got punished with guilt for having the abortion, and punished by Brad not talking to me or seeing me because I told him. I hope all this goes away soon. There is only so much I can deal with. Eventually, I am just going to flip on Brad.

July 1, 2008

Dear Diary,

I finally heard from Brad today. My morning started out like one of those days where you should have just stayed in bed. Then out of the blue, a message from Brad came through on my cell phone. The biggest smile came over my face as I read it. He wanted me to meet him at this little corner bar called Jack's Tavern for drinks later that evening. *Finally,* I thought, *he is back to the Brad I fell in love with.* I wish I could say it was that easy, but that's not the way it went.

I went shopping for a new outfit, then got my hair and nails done. I figured that I would look really pretty for Brad since he hadn't seen me in a while. I wanted him to see what he was missing. I purchased this tight-fitting red cocktail dress from Ashley Stewart. I had on red stilettos without pantyhose. I must say, I was looking hot. I waited until five to seven to leave my house. Brad told me to meet him at seven. This way, if Brad was going to be late again, I wouldn't be waiting too long.

I was so nervous when I reached the bar. There were a few guys standing outside with their cigarettes, blowing smoke all over the place. I walked into the bar to see if Brad was inside waiting for me. Of course he wasn't there yet. I went back outside to wait for him. The few guys who had been out here moments before went back inside, so it was just me standing out there alone as the sky became darker. I stood out there for about an hour. The sky was completely black. I looked up to see if there were any stars. When I turned my face up, rain fell from the dark sky. I ran back into the bar and found a deserted corner at the end of the bar. I sat there to wait for Brad.

Tears filled my eyes as I realized I may have been stood up again. I ordered a dry martini to pass the time, hoping he would eventually show. After the third drink, I texted him to see if he was held up. No response, so I called his phone. It went straight to voice mail. I waited a half hour with one more martini before I texted again. Finally, he responded. He had the nerve, after having me wait all this time for him, to say he wasn't coming because he had to work. Are you fucking kidding me? He was really going to keep me waiting and not cancel or tell me he had no intention on coming to meet me?

My blood was boiling now. I wanted to cry, scream, go to his house and bitch. I didn't know what to think or how to react. I hated to think he was doing this as some kind of payback toward me. If this was the game he was going to play, then why did he even apologize in the first place? I have no clue what is going on here or what his intentions are, but I will find out.

It hurts me so much that Brad would act as he is. I love this man so much, and for him not to forgive me after being honest with him breaks my heart. I have to fix this, no matter how long it takes. I'm just not sure how to approach him, considering I can't get him to talk to me. Then again, I know Brad will come around and start to miss me. Once he contacts me to apologize, just like last time, I will talk with him then. I'll give him the space he needs for now. If you love someone, let them go and they will find their way back. Isn't that what they say?

I hope all this blows over soon, really soon. It takes everything I have to resist calling him or texting. I think about him all the time and need to be with him every minute of every day. You'll see, we'll be together shortly. This time it'll be forever. Then we will start a family and live happily ever after.

15

July 12, 2008

Dear Diary,

Tell me why Brad texted me today. He was like, "Hey baby." I was thrilled to hear from him. Thank god, he has finally come to reason. I responded calmly: "Oh hi. How are you?" Do you know this S.O.B. had the nerve to ask who it was texting him? Are you fucking kidding me? He is going to play that game. Oh, hell no! I texted back, "This is Sandra. What, you forgot me already?" He was like, "No, I was just messing with you." What a relief, I thought. Brad was back to his old self again.

Or so I thought. He never texted back after that. I tried to text him many times after, but no response. I called his phone twice, and nothing. That's it, I've had enough. I'll give it a few days, and then I am going to his house. He'll have to talk to me if I'm standing in front of him. I am not waiting until he is ready to come around and talk to me. Now I'm calling the shots. In the meantime,

I will continue to call him and see if he answers the phone or texts me.

I think it will all work out between us if we sit down and talk everything out like two adults. Communication is the biggest part of relationships. We need to open up with one another to make this work out in the long run. At least, doing it this way, he'll see that I am very dedicated to him, and that I am willing to try to make it work through anything. I will give him the benefit of the doubt before going to his house. If he answers my calls or responds to my texts, then I'll work it out that way. I'll just prepare ahead of time for plan B, which is going to his house. I know that's what it's coming down to. I have to think about what I am going to say. That way I won't be nervous and stuttering.

July 20, 2008

Dear Diary,

That's it. I have been calling him and texting for five days, and nothing. So I got the courage up to go to his house. The whole way there, I played the conversation in my head over and over. I knew exactly what I wanted to say and how I wanted to say it. The closer to his house I got, the bigger the knot in my stomach became. I was trying so hard not to be nervous, but I couldn't help it. I was shaking, and I had the taste of vomit in my mouth.

I reached the door and rang the bell while

swallowing the lump in my throat. I was so nervous, I was sweating. No response to the first ring, so I tried again. I waited ten minutes, then I called his phone. I must have dialed the wrong number, because the operator came on the line saying the number was disconnected. I tried three more times and still got the operator.

He disconnected his phone and didn't tell me. How shallow could he be? Did this mean he didn't want to talk to me anymore? I can't believe this. He could have told me not to bother with him anymore. But no, he let me find out this way. What a coward he turned out to be. I was devastated. I slowly walked down the steps of his apartment and made my way home. With each step I took, another tear fell. My heart was broken, and only Brad could heal it.

Why did I let it go this far? If only I had been honest from the beginning, this would have never happened. What am I going to do now? I have nothing without Brad Clark. He is my everything, and now I am nothing. Was Brad trying to tell me that it was over, but he didn't have the balls to tell me in person? If so, he had definitely changed over the past couple of weeks.

Just when I thought my day couldn't get any worse, I received a letter in the mail. I had a bad feeling about the letter sticking out of the mailbox, considering there wasn't a return address on it. I headed straight to my room and put it on my desk. I wasn't going to pay it any mind. A while later, I decided to read the letter after all. I wish

I had just left this letter in the mailbox. It was a letter from Brad.

He started by telling me how he had feelings for me that I never showed him in return. I never told him how I felt. He said I dazzled him from the start, and he showed me his love in many ways but felt nothing. He wanted to know if I loved him, and if so, why didn't I tell him or show him. The devastating part came next. He said that he asked himself why he was with me. The more he questioned, the more he pulled away from me. Especially after what I had done, he knew it was over right then and there. He said he had a hard time letting me go. *Oh please,* I thought. Was that the purpose of his apology?

Then he got into how he lied to me about working. *Are you kidding me?* I thought. All this time he said he was working or busy, he was out with someone else. After all that bullshit, he tried covering his ass with, "I'll never forget you, and you deserve better. You'll always have a place in my heart." Did he think I would fall for that line of shit? Why would you say all this in a letter? What happened to being a man and speaking face to face? I have to say, I am heartbroken over all this. I was supposed to be his everything, not some whore off the street.

Despite the way I am feeling right now, I still want to be with him. I know if I can talk to him face to face, he will overlook this little incident. In return, I'll explain why I didn't open up to him. Hopefully he'll come to his senses. But how am I going to get him to talk with me? He disconnected his phone. I was thinking of showing up at his place every day until he answers the door. This way he'll have to talk to me. I don't care how long it takes, call me crazy, a stalker, whatever, I will have my man. Hell, it's not over until I say it's over.

August 9, 2008

Dear Diary,

Oh my god, Brad was telling the truth. I've gone to his house every day since that letter arrived, and today was the first time I saw him. As I made my way across the street, there he stood—with her. I froze. He was with that someone else he mentioned in his letter. They were arm in arm, hugging, kissing, and laughing. I watched them until the knot in my stomach climbed into my throat. Tears filled my eyes as I turned and walked away. I have no life without that man. What am I going to do now?

I must go back to his house and try to catch Brad alone so we can talk things over before he makes any serious decisions. I know Brad is stressed and probably feels like I deceived him. Although I made a mistake, I know I can fix this. After all, how long can you punish someone for an honest mistake? It's not like I intended for all this to happen as it did.

August 28, 2008

Dear Diary,

That's it! I give up! Brad is still with that whore of a girl. I went to Brad's house a few more times. Every time I went there, there they were, happily together. It reminded me of how happy Brad and I were—until he threw me out like a piece of garbage. Was this his way of showing me love—flaunting this girl in front of me? Fine. If that's how he wants to play, let the games begin. I have a few ideas of my own for how to get back at him. Maybe I'll write him a letter, or maybe I'll say something to his whore. Yeah, I'll tell this girl that Brad is still in love with me, and he is just using her for a piece of ass. What would she say to that? Maybe I should approach them both, and then we can talk like adults. Just the three of us, one big happy family. Ha, imagine that. Maybe that's what I will do after all. Why should Brad walk away from me and be happy about it? After the way he broke my heart, he deserves a little misery in his life.

Even after all this, would you believe I am still in love with him? I can't help it; I love him. Hell, if I thought it would work, I would go begging for Brad to take me back. Call me desperate, but I would. Then he would see how much I love him, how much I need him to be with me. Hey, anything is possible if you have faith. Brad and I were born to be together.

16

September 15, 2008

Dear Diary,

I can't take this anymore. Everywhere I turn, I see the two of them. They walk around this town like they are in their own world. I'm not even trying to be bothered by them anymore. I figured eventually I'll see Brad alone and that would be my chance to talk to him. But no, they are everywhere I go. I feel like I am being haunted by their love affair. The supermarket, the café where Brad and I used to go, the park—they are everywhere. How can I move on when I am constantly being reminded of how easily I have been replaced? It feels like Brad is just throwing this girl up in my face, as if to say, "Ha ha, she is better than you."

This bitch is not better than me, that's for sure. I am the who belongs with Brad Clark, not her. I've tried so hard to erase him from my thoughts, and I can't. And now she is in my thoughts with him. When I close my eyes, I can see the two of them kissing. That should be me with him in my own thoughts. I think of him making love to her the way he used to with me, and I get sick to my stomach. I didn't even get the chance to explain myself.

Everyone deserves a second chance. Where is mine? It's like he was in my life one minute and then gone the next. He never even looked back. He just erased everything he knew about me and called it a day. If this is how he wants it, then so be it. I'll eliminate myself from his life so he and his whore can live a horrible life together. We'll see how happy he is without me.

I can't live without Brad, and I won't. I'll never stop loving him. Brad moved on and did what he had to. Now it is time I do what I have to. I've thought about it for a while, and it's the only way I know how to deal with the pain that lingers in my heart. At least I can have the happy times I spent with Brad forever in my thoughts.

September 25, 2008

Dear Diary,

I am going to a place where I wish you not to follow. I will say good-bye today, as I will no longer be here tomorrow. I will hold you with me as I part from this world, for I no longer wish to live a foolish girl. All I had to do was say I love you; instead, I chose not to. He did what he had to. Forgive me for the sins I have done, as a new journey for me has begun.

I'll hold the words of love and hate with a

picture that holds my faith. I'll drink water mixed with pills to sleep; never to wake is the secret I keep. No time to say good-bye, for the minutes are fading fast. Everything I say now will soon be the past. My breaths are shallow, my heart is broken; I say farewell, for I must go. And now my eyes are starting to close.

Shaking her head from side to side, Laney closed the diary. "If only I knew what was going on, I could have helped her, and she would still be alive. Why, Sandra, why didn't you tell me?" Laney said out loud. As she put the diary down on the coffee table, a piece of paper fell to the floor. Curious, Laney picked it up. It was a letter from Sandra.

Dear Laney,

If you're reading this letter, then I have passed on. I see you found my diary. Please understand that I didn't mean to keep Brad Clark a secret. I guess I was afraid that if I exposed Brad, he would fade away. You know, kind of like a dream. I thought it was the right thing at the time, but I was wrong.

Because of my selfishness, I have faded from him. Now he wishes to marry another. I am devastated. I love him with all my heart, but I never confessed it to him. I wanted to make sure it was the right time to say it. Trust me, if I could change the way I did things, I would in a heartbeat. I should have been honest from the start.

Laney, promise me something. Promise me that when you fall in love with someone, you will be honest and true to them. You don't want to make the same mistake I did. Just remember, let you be loved before loving another. Love is an addiction we have no control over. It can make you do crazy things.

I know I will not be there for you physically, but I will always remain in your heart. Don't feel like I let you down by not being there for you. One more thing, Laney: no matter where life takes you, tell me everything that goes on. When you fall in love, tell me. When you get married, take me along. And when you have a baby, if it is a girl, will you name her after me?

Keep me in your heart, and I will always be close to you. I know we started off as friends; to tell you the truth, I saw you as the sister I never had. I am so sorry for not telling you anything. I know one day you will forgive me for your finding out what happened this way. I have to go now. Good-bye, Laney.

Love always,
Sandra

Laney lost control and let the tears fall. They fell hard. Laney dropped the letter and held a throw pillow tightly as she cried. By the time she stopped, much later, her head was pounding and she was hyperventilating. She ran to the bathroom. Laney cried so much she made herself throw up. She rinsed her face with cold water and rinsed out her mouth. She went into the kitchen and picked up the phone.

Laney dialed Scott's number. After three rings, a comforting voice answered. "Hello," Scott said in a sleepy voice.

"Scott, it's me, Laney. I need you to come over here immediately." Laney responded in one breath.

"Um, okay. What's the matter? Are you all right?" a sleepy Scott said.

"Yeah, everything is fine. I just have something to tell you, and I can't wait until the morning. You need to know now." Laney hung up.

Laney was so nervous waiting for Scott to arrive. In the meantime, she put the letter from Sandra back in the diary and hid them both in the top drawer of her dresser. It was best that Scott didn't know about the diary, she thought.

It wasn't long before Scott arrived and her bell was ringing. Butterflies had taken over Laney's stomach, but she opened the door. Scott stood in the doorway for a moment wearing a faded T-shirt with sweats, white sneakers, and a baseball cap. He looked cute that way, Laney thought.

Laney grabbed Scott and kissed him. It was a deep, passionate kiss. Then she pulled away. Once

Scott caught his breath, he said, "Wow, what was that for?"

"I need to be honest with you. I am so in love with you. I have been in love with you my whole life. I think about you all the time. I get nervous when I'm with you. And I had to tell you, before it was too late," Laney said all in one breath.

Scott looked at her as if he was deep in thought and stared at her for a moment. Then he scooped her up in his arms and looked into her eyes. "I've always loved you, and now that I know you feel the same way about me, I don't have to fight my feelings anymore when I am around you." Then he kissed her as she had kissed him moments before.

Some Time Later

Scott ended up staying with Laney the night of their first kiss and their confession of love. Laney changed her mind about moving back home, and Scott moved in with her the next day. It has been four years, and they have been together ever since. Their love has only grown stronger than the day before.

One day, Scott returned home from a three-day business trip with a big surprise for Laney. She ran into his arms, and they held each other for about five minutes. Then Scott got down on one knee and exposed a heart-shaped, two-carat diamond ring. He grabbed Laney's hand and asked for her hand in marriage. She accepted with delight and kissed him. He kissed her in return, and the passion between them just got stronger and stronger.